SPECIAL MESSAGE TO READERS

This book is published under the auspices of

THE ULVERSCROFT FOUNDATION

(registered charity No. 264873 UK)

Established in 1972 to provide funds for research, diagnosis and treatment of eye diseases.

Examples of contributions made are: —

A Children's Assessment Unit at Moorfield's Hospital, London.

•

Twin operating theatres at the Western Ophthalmic Hospital, London.

•

A Chair of Ophthalmology at the Royal Australian College of Ophthalmologists.

•

The Ulverscroft Children's Eye Unit at the Great Ormond Street Hospital For Sick Children, London.

You can help further the work of the Foundation by making a donation or leaving a legacy. Every contribution, no matter how small, is received with gratitude. Please write for details to:

THE ULVERSCROFT FOUNDATION,
The Green, Bradgate Road, Anstey,
Leicester LE7 7FU, England.
Telephone: (0116) 236 4325

In Australia write to:

THE ULVERSCROFT FOUNDATION,
c/o The Royal Australian and New Zealand College of Ophthalmologists,
94-98 Chalmers Street, Surry Hills,
N.S.W. 2010, Australia

THE LOST FILES OF SHERLOCK HOLMES

Dr John Watson finally reopens the lid of his old tin dispatch box and unearths a veritable treasure trove of unpublished tales recounting the remarkable skills of his friend and colleague, Mr Sherlock Holmes. With the detective's consent, we are now finally privileged to witness how Holmes, with his customary brilliance, unravelled the secrets lurking within a too-perfect police constable, a Colonel with a passion for Arthurian mythology, and the public house which never sold a single pint of ale . . .

Books by Paul D. Gilbert
in the Linford Mystery Library:

THE CHRONICLES OF
SHERLOCK HOLMES

PAUL D. GILBERT

THE LOST FILES OF SHERLOCK HOLMES

Complete and Unabridged

LINFORD
Leicester

First published in Great Britain
by Robert Hale Limited, London

First Linford Edition
published 2009
by arrangement with
Robert Hale Limited, London

British Library CIP Data

Gilbert, Paul D. (Paul David), *1954* –
The lost files of Sherlock Holmes.- -
(Linford mystery library)
1. Holmes, Sherlock (Fictitious character)- - Fiction.
2. Watson, John H. (Fictitious character)- - Fiction.
3. Detective and mystery stories, English.
4. Large type books.
I. Title II. Series
823.9′2–dc22

ISBN 978–1–84782–910–8

Published by
F. A. Thorpe (Publishing)
Anstey, Leicestershire

Set by Words & Graphics Ltd.
Anstey, Leicestershire
Printed and bound in Great Britain by
T. J. International Ltd., Padstow, Cornwall

This book is printed on acid-free paper

For: my sorely missed parents and
our dear cousin Jane

Special thanks to my many close and supportive family and friends, and of course to Andrew Hills, and my darling Jackie, who have cleared so many stones from my path

Foreword

As the more avid among my, thankfully, many readers will have observed over the years, it has been with extreme difficulty that I have striven to apply chronology to the narratives concerning my good friend Mr Sherlock Holmes and his amazing powers of deduction.

It has been equally arduous to obtain his approval, for my humble literary efforts, and, indeed, his permission for me to publish them. However, over the years, I have managed to extricate various case notes from my metal box, secured within the vaults of Cox's & Co. Bank and Holmes has allowed me to feed them slowly to my public.

Those examples that have, hitherto, remained within the box have been held back for a variety of reasons. Some for reasons of diplomacy, others because of the pain their publication might have caused to those people directly involved at the time of their occurrence, and there are those that Holmes insisted remain unpublished for his own personal reasons. The category that each story falls into will become apparent upon being read.

That these tales have now seen the light of day at all can be attributed to a short, terse message that I received a few months ago, from Holmes at his Sussex retreat. It read as follows:

My Dear Watson
I trust you are well and that your practice still flourishes. Should you and your readers still be interested in the career of an inadequate, retired amateur detective, I now see no reason why you should not delve once more into your damnable metal box and release those tales which to date you have so obligingly withheld. While I admit that I still do not share the enthusiasm of either you, or your readers, for such things it might be amusing to see these in print at long last. I look forward to your next visit

to my humble country abode, whereupon I might peruse your scribblings.

Yours SH.

I smiled at Holmes's self-deprecating humour, but could not help but wonder at the chain of thought that had prompted his message to me. This, I was sure, I would never discover, notwithstanding that, however, I wasted no time in reclaiming my box from its vault and set to reassembling my notes into some sort of coherent order before Holmes had a chance to change his mind once more.

These stories have not been released in any form of chronology, nor in an order of priority. They are simply, further examples of the powers and rare gifts with which my good friend, Mr Sherlock Holmes, has been endowed.

J. H. WATSON.

The Adventure of the Connoisseur

'There is something almost soothing in the gentle line of the brush strokes of the great impressionist artists,' Holmes began, most surprisingly, after breakfast on a bright spring morning. I say surprisingly because in all the years of our association this was the first occasion on which he had initiated a conversation on the arts.

Still more surprising was his affable, almost cheerful mood for it had been some weeks since the last noteworthy problem had been concluded and normally a long period of inactivity produced in Holmes a dark, brooding malaise.

Scanning the all too familiar walls of our sitting room, Holmes continued, 'The simple beauty of Renoir, the clever use of colour of Monet, totally different in style, yet somehow embodying the same love of nature. Our room could certainly benefit from the addition of some pictures, eh Watson?'

I was so astonished by this line of conversation that I could not, for the life of me, think of any sort of reply. I, instead, lit a cigarette and studied my friend's countenance. For a brief instant a mocking, almost mischievous smile played on Holmes's lips and by applying his own methods, I reached my conclusion.

'You have a case,' I blurted out, 'involving an artist or art dealer!'

Lighting his after-breakfast pipe, Holmes replied, 'My dear Watson, you absolutely scintillate at this early hour.' As he said this he tossed me a white printed calling card.

As I took the card, I could not help smiling at his use of the word 'early' for it was just past the hour of ten. It was true to say, however, that when not gainfully employed, Holmes kept most Bohemian hours and my own schedule did not preclude me from keeping them also.

The size of the card was standard, the print, sharp, black italic. It announced a Nathaniel Graves of the 'Reform and

Connoisseur Clubs, Montpelier Square'. On the reverse had been written, in neat precise handwriting, 'an eleven o'clock appointment would be most convenient'.

'Mr Graves is obviously not a man who bandies words or begs favours, merely a statement of fact and not a request. Yet how can you be so sure he wishes to consult you on a matter concerning art?' I asked.

'Bottom of column four, page six,' Holmes replied, as he threw across a badly mangled copy of *The Times*. A tiny article provided me with my answer.

It described, in the barest detail, an art theft from a town house in Montpelier Square, belonging to a renowned connoisseur and collector.

'It says here,' I read aloud, '*The only item missing from an otherwise fine and balanced collection, was a relatively worthless landscape*. You surprise me, Holmes, the theft of so insignificant an item is hardly to your taste.'

'Yet a man of his obvious standing in the art world wishes to consult me on this matter. There is the minutest of difference between value and worth, Watson. The fact that Nathaniel Graves attaches value to an item of little worth, will, I trust, provide us with a most singular little problem. Come now! We barely have time to dress before our appointment.'

'Our appointment?' I queried, taking Holmes to task, once again, for taking my assistance for granted.

'Assuming, of course, you will honour me with your valuable expertise and experience in this matter. If however any pressing matters at your surgery prevent your participation . . . ' Despite the half mocking tone of his voice, I needed to hear no more.

'No, not at all, things have been quiet of late and I should be delighted to assist you in any way that I can.' So, laughing, we both went off to dress.

The entrance of Nathaniel Graves, shown upstairs by Mrs Hudson, took us both aback, not only by his precise punctuality, it was exactly eleven o'clock, but also by his striking appearance. For there, standing before us, was the very embodiment of middle-class, late Victorian austerity.

He stood around six foot two inches, but was made to look taller by his slimness of build and the lines of his black frock coat. His features were rigid and stern, his brow prematurely furrowed for a man in his early forties, his nose and chin were both prominent and strong. To complete this picture, his black shoes and tall hat shone brilliantly and spoke clearly of his position and rank in society.

'Mr Holmes?' He glanced disdainfully at my friend, his speech clipped and precise, his lips barely moving. Holmes nodded and politely showed our client to a chair.

'I should rather stand. Now I will not bandy words, Mr Holmes, I shall state my intentions clearly and precisely from the outset. I want this matter cleared up as quickly as possible with little or no publicity . . . '

'Mr Graves!' Holmes shouted, 'I am not in the habit of raising my voice unduly, nor of being dictated to in such a manner, especially by a stranger whose case I have not yet agreed to undertake. Assuming I do, I shall require clear, precise facts and information, not demands.'

Graves was clearly taken aback by this outburst, for his white face visibly reddened and his furrows deepened.

'Well I don't know, I must say!' Graves protested. 'I am not accustomed to being addressed in such a fashion.'

'That, indeed, is a wonder in itself,' Holmes retorted, turning his back on Graves and taking up a position by the window.

Clearly determined to engage Holmes's services at whatever cost, Graves collected himself.

'Now, look Mr Holmes, there is no need to carry on so, really there is not. I simply wish to make my position clear from the outset.'

This drew no response from Holmes, who still had his back to Graves.

'I can assure you, I employ investigators all the time in my line of work, it is just that in matters of a personal nature, I require the best. Nonetheless, I shall seek assistance elsewhere if need be.' At this Graves put on his hat and turned to leave.

I was sure that Graves's last comment

would appeal to Holmes's delight as a compliment and his natural vanity, which at times he took small pains to conceal. A slight smile played on his lips, which told me my judgement was a correct one. He turned towards us once more.

'Mr Graves, kindly provide me with the details of your strange theft,' he said quietly. 'That you are a successful solicitor, who specialises in company law, I am in little doubt, the other details I shall require from you,' Holmes added, nonchalantly.

'I am at a loss as to how you reached your conclusion, I really cannot tell,' Graves said returning once more to the centre of the room.

'Yes really, Holmes!' I began, also at a loss.

'Tut, tut, come, Watson.'

Reluctantly Holmes explained. 'The briefcase you left by the door is one most commonly used by men of the law. Your company address, inscribed faintly on the back of your card, is a side street to the rear of Threadneedle Street, an area that proliferates in bankers and solicitors, yet,

I have not heard, to date, of a banker who employs investigators. The fact that you have accrued sufficient wealth to enable you to collect art at so young an age indicates that you are not a run-of-the-mill conveyancer, therefore, you are involved in the City.' Holmes shrugged, as if this should have been as clear to me also and was pleased to note that Graves was suitably impressed.

'I must confess, your reputation does not seem to be entirely unfounded,' Graves offered reluctantly.

'Ha! A fine compliment indeed!' Holmes exclaimed. 'Now the details of this robbery of yours please . . .'

'Mr Holmes, as you so correctly concluded, my years in the City have not been financially unkind to me. I have always worked diligently and am also gratified to note that during these years and the hundreds of transactions I have been a part of, I have accrued a reputation for honesty and straight dealing. Though, not unique, such a reputation in this day and age is somewhat of a rarity and therefore something to be cherished by the holder of such and sought after by those seeking his advice. Without wishing to sound conceited, it is true to say that, as a consequence of this, a successful future in my career is now assured me.

'On the basis of this solid foundation, I now feel able to indulge my only passion in life, namely the acquisition of fine works of art. To be frank, gentlemen, though I am a great admirer of beauty and the skills of a great artist, the collecting of pictures is not for me at least, purely aesthetic, it is also a sound investment.

'I do not merely purchase and hoard. When I feel the time is right, I will sell a work, which I consider has reached the zenith of its value. Therefore, I study the works of new and rising artists, make a purchase relatively cheaply and bide my time. Thankfully, I have enjoyed some success in my art ventures and now command a certain respect amongst gallery owners and other dealers.

'The point I am making, gentlemen, is that while these peripheral works are continually coming and going, the core of my collection, those works whose value I can never see declining, is comprised of the choicest paintings. I possess, for example, a fine example of Goya and a magnificent Fragonard. The only exception was the stolen picture, an insignificant and worthless landscape, the value of which was purely of personal sentiment.'

At this Holmes's eyes, previously languid and bereft of emotion, suddenly burst into life and he leaned forward, fingertips pressed together.

'A point that is immediately suggestive, wouldn't you say, Watson?'

'Oh indeed,' I confirmed, but without my friend's enthusiasm.

'I find your levity somewhat surprising, Mr Holmes,' Graves began. 'Whilst this business may strike you as a trifling matter, I can assure you I do not share your opinion. The landscape is reminiscent of my first home, but, that aside, a crime has been committed and being a servant of the law, I intend to see justice done, at whatever cost and inconvenience.'

'Well said indeed, Mr Graves, but your impressions of my own feelings on the matter are entirely erroneous. I very much doubt that this affair is at all trifling, equally, I feel we must act with all speed. Therefore Watson and I will join you at your home at six o'clock this evening, where, I trust, you will describe the circumstances of the theft. In the meantime, if you will furnish me with the name of the gallery where you purchased the picture, I will pursue my enquiries in the interim period. Good day, sir.'

At that, Holmes strode to the mantelpiece, picked out his cherry wood and began filling it with tobacco from the Persian slipper, whilst I, in turn, ushered the bemused connoisseur through the door.

'Really, Holmes, considering the dearth of noteworthy problems we are experiencing at present, I consider your behaviour towards Mr Graves to be most off-hand, almost downright rude!' My indignation was wasted, however, for, as I turned from the door, I observed my friend sitting cross legged on his chair, eyes closed, arms folded, whilst endless streams of smoke drifted from his pipe. Whatever thoughts or reasoning had triggered this deep contemplation of his, there was little doubt that this would continue for some time and any further attempts at conversation would be futile.

I sat, for the next hour, in a somewhat disgruntled mood, scanning my paper, without digesting its contents. The occasional glance I might shoot at Holmes from behind my paper, revealed no change in his attitude or position. Indeed, as his pipe died away, the unknowing observer might have presumed that he was asleep.

I was in the process of lighting my own second pipe when a most piercing cry from Holmes prompted me to drop the unlit pipe altogether.

'Watson! We will not resolve this matter by sitting around here all day, I am off to Wesbourne Park Grove. Please be at Graves's home promptly at six o'clock. Our new client seems to value punctuality.'

'Am I to be redundant then, all afternoon?' I asked, not intending to hide my hurt feelings.

'Not at all, old fellow, your task is to locate and employ a talented landscape artist, and ensure he is with us at Montpelier Square this evening. Come along, Watson.' He cajoled me into action. It was a strange task he had set for me, but resolving to begin my enquiries at a college of art, I pursued Holmes from the room at all speed. We snatched our hats as we careered down to the street to find our cabs, almost injuring Mrs Hudson as we did so.

The profusion of aspiring landscape artists yet to be discovered and consequently, near to starvation, made my task far easier than I would have expected, so my offer of a commission, despite its modesty, was eagerly accepted. I chose a dark-haired young man, in his early twenties, whose intentness of observation and open smile, belied his ragged attire and unshaven face. The samples of his work, that had escaped his discontented destruction, convinced me of his talent. Consequently, we arrived at Montpelier Square some twenty minutes before the appointed hour.

I put this time to good use by inviting the young man, who went by the name of Timothy Ryan, to do a rough sketch of Montpelier Square itself. Initially I was disappointed that the task was completed in so short a time, we still had ten minutes before our expected arrival, but this was transformed into amazement when I observed the accuracy, detail and beautiful effect that Ryan had achieved.

Montpelier Square was a typical example of the modern, inner-suburban back streets, built specifically for the newly wealthy, who required easy access to the City, but had taste and class enough to demand a quiet, more genteel home environment than was available in a more cramped central position.

The lines of the houses were simple, but dignified, exuding an impression of wealth, without being austere. Trees lined the Square in abundance and small front lawns were visible behind the lush greenery of mature hedges and lilac trees.

We ascended a short flight of steps and rang the bell, which was answered by a petite young maid. We were shown into a large, airy, drawing-room, its walls adorned by a large number of fine oil paintings, as one would have expected.

Ryan examined each painting in turn, scornful of some, wistfully envious of others, whilst I was merely awestruck by their beauty. At precisely six o'clock the chimes of a large, elegant carriage clock announced the arrival of our host. His tall, severe, figure seemed to cast an air of tension over the previously relaxed atmosphere.

'Gentlemen,' he said, disdainfully, gazing down the full length of his nose at the dishevelled Ryan. 'I see your colleague is late, Dr Watson, I trust this does not reflect on the precision of his work.'

I assured him it did not, and that I was sure he would be but a few moments. In this I proved to be inaccurate and noticed Graves become increasingly agitated. Indeed, we waited twenty minutes before the bell at the front door sounded again. The icy glare that greeted the arrival of my friend would have frozen the blood of many a business adversary or unco-operative client, but not Sherlock Holmes. He raced into the room, a positive gleam in his eye, and stole a questioning glance towards Ryan.

'Timothy Ryan, the artist,' I replied to his unspoken query.

'You have surely surpassed yourself, Watson,' he exclaimed, rubbing his long sinewy hands together, 'and now I should be glad to view your gallery, Mr Graves. I take it, it is on the upper floor?' He spoke these last few words as he hurried from the room.

'Well, upon my word,' Graves protested. 'This will not do. This will not do at all.'

I merely shrugged. 'The gallery then?' I suggested.

Slowly, reddening with suppressed rage, Graves tightened his thin, colourless lips and strode from the room, Ryan and I following closely behind.

'I have enjoyed a most productive afternoon,' Holmes announced to me as soon as we had gained entrance into the gallery, which, as Holmes had correctly surmised, was situated in an airy, well lit room on the uppermost floor.

'So I perceive,' I said attempting to suppress my own indignation at his repeatedly shoddy treatment of our client. Holmes had, however, detected my anger but merely laughed.

'Oh Watson, you should know my methods well enough by now.'

At this, Holmes halted, for he had just noticed an area of wall, approximately three foot square, where the previous presence of a painting was obvious by the discolouration of the wall.

In an instant, Holmes was lying on his stomach, scanning the large, rich Persian carpet with his lens. He was as dexterous in this position as a snake seeking its prey, and repeatedly a cry of triumph, occasionally, a groan of dismay, sounded from the floor. On one occasion I noticed him extract a small particle of dust, or even, ash, with a fingernail. This he examined minutely. Then, finally he dusted this away and leaped to his feet like a recoiling spring.

'My examination of this room has been most informative, and confirms the evidence I received at the gallery this afternoon. Yet, I fancy the height of this floor will have prevented the thief from making his entrance up here.'

'The thief gained access through the window of the first floor parlour, the security of which I have, to date, unfortunately, neglected,' Graves reluctantly informed us.

'Unfortunate indeed!' Holmes gravely observed. 'I should like to examine this window if I may.'

'Very well, but I cannot see where all this tomfoolery is getting you.'

Holmes however was already descending the stairway to the first floor, leaving us there in his wake and still none the wiser.

By the time we had reached the parlour, Holmes had all but concluded his examination of the window and sill and gestured us to be seated before him.

'My already tenuous indulgence is now done to exhaustion, Mr Holmes,' Graves announced. 'This leaping about the room like some jack-in-the-box does not impress me a jot.'

Holmes was arrogantly dismissive of

these protestations from Graves, regarding, as he often did, his client merely as his introduction to his own private contest with the elusive truth. That he was now close to this truth was evident to me at least, in the certain gleam of his eye and a strange half smile that would not be subdued.

'The tangled strands of this case have provided me with a wealth of deductive and analytical opportunities which I could hardly have expected from such a seemingly, innocuous burglary. Yet my investigations and deductions have led me to a conclusion that seems to satisfy all the facts.

'It is to be hoped that you, Mr Ryan, will provide me with the final clue, with Mr Graves' co-operation and enable us to bring this affair to its natural conclusion.'

'It is still a mystery to me why this scoundrel is in my house at all, much less how he can possibly be of any assistance,' Graves snarled, peering down his nose once more.

'By sketching an exact duplication of the missing painting,' Holmes continued quickly, before Graves could resume his tiresome jibes. 'The possibility that the theft of a relatively worthless painting, in the midst of such artistic treasures, could have been a mishap born of ignorance did occur to me initially. My examination of this parlour window, however, indicates that an experienced professional had been at work. Such an expert would hardly have preferred a nondescript landscape over, say, the Goya, unless there was a far deeper motive for its theft.

'The owner of the gallery, from which you made the purchase, paid a heavy price for violating the artist's instructions to him. I understand you persuaded him to sell the painting to you rather than to the person that had originally ordered it, by almost doubling the asking price?' Holmes queried.

'Indeed I did, yet it was still only a trifling amount when weighed against the pleasure gained from the reminiscences that it provided. A heavy price you say?'

'Alas, yes. The anger of the intended buyer was such that the hapless gallery owner was hospitalised for some time, the marks of the injuries to his face and head still most evident. Yet he was able to provide me with the name and whereabouts of the artist.'

'Indeed, so at least some progress is being made,' Graves conceded.

'Most definitely. The individual in question is one James Tyler, currently enjoying accommodation at Her Majesty's pleasure in Wormwood Scrubs, having committed a most violent robbery. Fortunately his victim survived and, for good behaviour, his governor has allowed him the privilege of oil and canvas, which, as you know, he has put to most excellent use.

'My further enquiries, at the Yard, have revealed the existence of an accomplice, in all probability his brother, John, who evaded capture and is still at large. Since the description of the gallery owner's assailant coincides with that of the Yard's description of John Tyler, there can be little doubt as for whom the painting was intended, nor, indeed, as to the perpetrator of your own theft. Doctor Watson and I will wait in another room, while you describe the missing picture to our friend Ryan, here.' Turning from Graves to Ryan, Holmes continued, 'Your commission, Mr Ryan, will not earn you a reputation in the art world, but the reward that might be forthcoming, will certainly start you on your way. Come, Watson.'

Leaving Graves and Ryan as bemused and taken aback as myself, I descended with Holmes to the ground-floor drawing-room to await the outcome of Ryan's artistic endeavours.

'I must say, Holmes, the rapidity with which you have solved this confounded mystery has surpassed many of your past achievements. I confess, however, that the nature of the importance these brothers attach to the picture and how Ryan's sketch will assist us is still a mystery to me.'

'The first point is obvious, Watson. The proceeds of Tyler's robbery were never recovered by the police, therefore it is a reasonable assumption to make that Tyler hid these prior to his arrest, without the knowledge of his brother. This landscape that he was so intent on his brother gaining possession of, is nothing more than an elaborate treasure map. I am certain that upon discovering the painting's secret we will unearth the booty, hopefully before Tyler does. The first step towards finding its location is a relatively easy one and one I am sure John Tyler will also be equal to.

'I discovered, from the unfortunate gallery owner, that the title of this painting is Bowen Bridge Farm. John Tyler's arrest took place just under thirty-six hours after the crime was committed. The robbery took place in North West London, therefore we must make enquiries at the Ministry of Agriculture and obtain a list of farms in the surrounding area. I should not be surprised if Bowen Bridge Farm appears as one of these.

'The exact location of the booty however, will, I fear, be harder to calculate and I merely hope it takes Tyler longer to work it out than me. Ha! Here comes our sketch.'

Having already witnessed the sketch

Ryan did of Montpelier Place in under ten minutes, I was not surprised to see that he had completed his task in such a short time. I was once more, awestruck at my friend's sharp, analytical mind at work.

'Excellent, Holmes!' I exclaimed, 'Once again your reasoning is amazingly sound.'

Graves caught my words as he and Ryan entered the room. 'That, sir, remains to be seen,' Graves remarked with disdain. 'Though what assistance this poor sketch will be to you, I really cannot tell!'

Holmes ignored Graves's comments once again. 'Come, Watson! Mr Graves, as and when we have news of your painting and its recovery, you shall be duly informed. Good-day to you.' So saying, Sherlock Holmes ushered Ryan and myself out into the gathering darkness.

After we had compensated Ryan with a most welcomly received five guineas, he went on his way. The interior of our cab was too dark, by this time, for us to study the sketch, but upon reaching 221b, we immediately turned up the gas and spread the picture flat on the table.

Though the technique was undoubtedly brilliant, the content was sadly lacking in any singular features and left me in grave doubt as to our ever being able to unlock its secret. The foreground featured a flat stretch of grass chewed by a pair of quite ordinary cows. To the left stood a large group of full-grown cherry trees and to the right stood a distant square-built farmhouse. In the central background were grouped three quite attractive small cottages, whilst the sky contained two lonely white clouds and a brace of swallow.

In silence we two leaned over the table for a full ten minutes till, despairing of ever discovering anything significant, I straightened myself and lit a cigarette.

'I am so sorry, Holmes,' I said by way of consolation. 'After so masterful a piece of deduction we appear to have run into a blind alley. I can see nothing in this sketch to draw our attention.'

I turned to my friend for confirmation, but instead found he had not heard a word I had said. His eyes had taken on a steely gaze, his features were quite inscrutable. In an instant he had snatched up the sketch and took it to his chair, in front of which he positioned a high-backed dining chair. On this he propped up the sketch.

Taking his tobacco from the Persian slipper, he lit up his black clay pipe and sitting cross-legged, his knees almost up to his chin, he stared at the picture, his eyes never once leaving the study of this drawing.

'Will you retire soon, Holmes?' I asked. 'A clear head in the morning may help to solve this puzzle.' The only reply was Holmes drawing long and hard on his shag and I reluctantly went to my room.

My anxiety for Holmes's well-being was not unfounded, for I found his position unchanged the following morning, only now his hair was in disarray, his complexion quite ashen and his eyes seemed heavy and lined with dark circles. His black clay pipe had evidently been discarded at some stage during his long night, for the floor about his chair was littered with the tiny butts of well smoked cigarettes.

'This is really inexcusable, Holmes! To abuse yourself so, for the sake of a solitary picture, a worthless one at that. You must take to your bed at once.'

Slowly Holmes raised his tired eyes towards me. 'There is considerably more at stake here than a mere landscape which, by the way, I am sure, will soon cease to exist. Tyler's robbery, which took place at a bank in Highgate, involved the death of a guard. Our real quarry, therefore, is an accessory to murder and our other priority, the recovery of the not inconsiderable proceeds.'

'Yes, but even so.'

'I trust you are ready for your visit to the ministry?' Holmes asked wearily.

'I am. I must insist, however, that you rest yourself at least while I am out.'

Holmes merely waved me away, with a languid, almost distorted movement of his hand and resumed his scrutiny of the sketch while lighting yet another cigarette.

Reluctantly and with a heavy heart I took my leave.

My morning's work was long and tiresome, the bureaucracy of the British Civil Service being as slow and clumsy as it is. Nonetheless, by lunch-time my efforts were at last rewarded and a smallholding, just north of Borehamwood, emerged as our likely destination.

I hurried back to Baker Street with my news, flushed with success. I found to my amazement that a miraculous transformation had come over Holmes. Gone was the dishevelled wreck I had left behind and there, dressed and ready for action, was the Holmes I knew only too well. Shaved and immaculate in black frock coat he smiled broadly as I entered, rubbing his hands contentedly together.

'The speed of your return and lightness of step upon the stairs indicate that you have been as successful as I. All we need now is your army revolver and we are ready for him!' Holmes's eyes glistened like a bird of prey and his mouth twitched with suppressed excitement.

'Oh, but surely you will explain your discovery before we leave.'

'Patience, my dear fellow. Pray furnish

me with the information that I still require,' he asked.

I informed Holmes of the farm's location and only once we had consulted our Bradshaw and confirmed that we had some two hours to spare before the departure of the next train to Borehamwood, did he consent to explain how matters really stood.

'Before we review the sketch for one last time, I must explain to you, Watson, that the matter uppermost in my mind is the apprehension of John Tyler. Though I am sure some manner of reward will be forthcoming should we prove to be successful, neither the recovery of the proceeds of the robbery, nor, indeed, the recovery of the painting itself, are my priorities. With that in mind I have placed an advertisement in all the popular newspapers to the effect that a Mr Tyler wishes to dispose of a pleasing cottage at Bowen Bridge Farm. I have little doubt that, assuming he can manage at all, lacking my own keen faculties, it will take Tyler considerably longer than me to unlock the secret of his brother's painting. By placing the advertisement in the morning's notices, we will have time enough to locate and recover the money at our leisure, then to remain at the cottage and be at hand for when Tyler finally makes his appearance,' Holmes concluded triumphantly.

'Splendid logic, as usual, Holmes, your trap seems well set, although you are assuming the cottage remains unoccupied.'

'Yes, but I feel it is a reasonable enough assumption to make. James Tyler would have established its long-term vacancy before depositing there all that he had risked so much to obtain. Now to the sketch.

'A subtle mind has James Tyler, and it is to the public good that such a mind, coupled with his own perverse ruthlessness, now lies incarcerated as opposed to being free to ply his vile and evil trade. As you can see, Watson, the number of potential hiding places is almost infinite, buried under the field, in or around the cottages, the trees, the list is endless. Yet there is one glaring anomaly, that really should have struck me immediately.'

'I must confess, Holmes, that none presents itself to me. All is peace, beauty and tranquillity, with not a hint of that which lies hidden.'

Obviously enjoying himself, Holmes rubbed his hands together, laughing aloud.

'I must give you a clue then, those great impressionist artists we were discussing the other morning, though differing greatly in style and technique, had one thing in common that distanced them from their somewhat ponderous predecessors. They all drew their inspiration from nature itself. That is what you must do now.'

'From nature?' I repeated under my breath. Holmes's clue aided me not at all. I studied the field once more and the trees, but the only conclusion I could draw was that the scene depicted was high summer. Some cherry trees in the painting held no blossom, were in full leaf with no sign of the early autumnal growth of cherries taking place as yet. I related this discovery to Holmes.

'Excellent, Watson, quite excellent,

though you have failed to observe the occasional brown patchy stains in the grass which not only indicate high summer, but that it has been a hot dry summer also. Why then is the chimney stack, of the centre cottage, billowing out smoke so profusely?'

'Tyler's clue, of course! Really, Holmes you have quite surpassed yourself throughout this case. I shall get my revolver.'

'If you would be so kind and I shall ask Mrs Hudson to call us a cab. We may just have time for a late lunch at the station before our train.'

Holmes was correct in his surmise, although our repast was somewhat hurried and our train's departure was prompt. In a short while the grime of London was behind us and I sat back contentedly, contemplating the rebirth of nature that occurs each spring. Every tree was showing signs of budding, blossom or even tiny leaves and the grass had a lush freshness about it. I thought, momentarily, of sharing this observation with my friend, but preferred silence to his inevitable rebuff. On more than one occasion in the past, he had voiced not only his indifference to such natural beauty, but also his conviction that the isolation of country living provided a veritable breeding ground for crime and undoubtedly in this instance, he had been proved correct.

'Watson,' he suddenly began, 'I take it you now share my view that the isolation of the Bowen Bridge cottage, and no other factor, rendered it a far easier location for the depositing of stolen goods than any urban area.'

He laughed at my startled expression and then explained.

'Really there is no cause for wonderment. It was obvious to me, from the contented expression on your face, and your reluctance in turning from it, that you were enjoying the scenic beauty we are passing through. When you did, however, it was only to glance quizzically in my direction and, no doubt remembering our recent conversation on the way to the 'Copper Beeches', you decided not to raise this topic of discussion. The fact that you did not, led me to my observation.'

'I cannot deny that you are correct in every detail, though my agreement with you applies to this case alone. I still contend that the everyday strife and squalor of London life is a far more profuse breeding ground for crime than the tranquillity of a country location.'

'Such as the 'Copper Beeches'?' he sarcastically asked.

Before I could protest, however, we began pulling into the station at Borehamwood and wasted no time in alighting and locating an available trap.

We were fortunate, indeed, in acquiring transport so readily outside a station as quiet and remote as Borehamwood and the driver, a large thickset man of middle years, with dark brooding eyes, was willing to assist us, knowing well the direction to our desired location.

We started off at a brisk pace, the large bay seeming fresh and healthy and the scenery seemed more stunning since leaving the speed of the train.

'Tell me, fellow,' Holmes broke the tranquil silence by addressing our driver and tapping him on the shoulder, 'have there been other recent visitors to the farm, perhaps expressing an interest in the vacant cottage?'

The driver seemed reluctant to answer, but when he did, it was with a strong East End accent. 'Nah, not as far as I know, suh, fings are pretty quiet 'ere abouts.'

Holmes grunted, content that we were still one step ahead of our adversary, though we were certain the advertisement would bring him to us soon enough. We concluded our journey in silence. Despite the changes brought about by the seasonal differences, the green of the grass and the blossoms on the many trees, Graves's landscape came to life as we approached and could see the farmhouse was indeed located two hundred yards, or so, from the cottages. Holmes asked the driver to wait for us and despatched me to the farmhouse to explain our intentions to the owner, while he began his inspection of the middle cottage.

I felt quite jaunty as I started up the long driveway. The air was invigorating and we were nearing the satisfactory conclusion of our problem. I struck out at a brisk pace and only turned back briefly when I heard the impatient whinnying of the bay mare. To my great astonishment, standing directly behind me was the very man who had driven our trap from the station. His friendly demeanour of before was now contorted by an evil, malicious, grimace etched into his soot-soiled face. In his right hand he wielded a ferocious cudgel, which he then raised above his head, in readiness to bring down upon my own. My solitary, futile act of resistance was to raise my arms to protect my crown from the impending impact.

Then, to my immense relief, I heard my army revolver being fired from a distance. For an agonizing moment, I feared that Holmes had missed his mark, for the man stood there still, his weapon poised above his head. However, I became aware of a deep red hole in the centre of his forehead, the cudgel fell from his lifeless grasp, and he slowly collapsed into the mud just yards away from the prize he had come so far to claim. To assure myself of the man's lack of threat, I grabbed hold of the cudgel before bending down to examine him for signs of life. There were none.

As I straightened up again I cast my gaze about me and saw Holmes running full pelt towards me from the direction of the centre cottage.

Breathlessly he exclaimed, 'Watson, my dear fellow! I trust you are unharmed?'

I nodded with a smile of affirmation, still unsure of the true meaning of these recent dramatic events. Then, to my surprise, Holmes prised the cudgel from my hand and crashed it repeatedly to the ground until it shattered into fragments.

'I curse my natural conceit for allowing this creature and his abominable weapon to threaten your life. The consequences had my timing and aim been less sure, are unthinkable. I owe you my humblest of apologies and yet I could not have been assured of Tyler betraying himself, had I not drawn him out by our separating.'

'You mean that you were aware of Tyler masquerading as our driver from the outset?' I asked in disbelief, at Holmes's flagrant abuse of me as his bait, once again.

'In truth, Watson, I had not anticipated Tyler arriving at Borehamwood prior to us. I am as guilty of underestimating his abilities, as I am of overestimating my own. However, upon boarding the cart, I was made immediately aware of my error and decided to allow him to play his hand, not realizing that he would be bold enough to play it so soon. Of course, I could not warn you of his rapid approach without warning him off and then our bird would have flown. Again, old friend, my apologies.' We began walking slowly towards the farmhouse, where we hoped to procure a lad to send to the village to summon the police and perhaps, a means of transport back to the station.

'At least now I understand why you allowed Tyler off the leash, but how did you realize he was anything other than a humble cart-driver?'

'I was alerted to the possibility as soon as we boarded the cart. I observed the cudgel lying on the floor at the front by his feet; a ferocious weapon, indeed, for a driver in so remote and quiet a village as Borehamwood. Then I became aware of how soiled by soot his face was. You would rarely find such soiling on any face other than one from an intensely built-up, urban area, such as East London, for example, from where Tyler surely hails, as confirmed by his accent. It was his hands, however, that decided me to borrow your revolver. On the hands of every driver that I have observed there are always obvious red welts caused by the strain of controlling the horse with the reins. On Tyler's there were none,' Holmes concluded.

'I understand, but how could you be so sure he would come after me and not yourself? Surely you were in the same danger as I was?' I asked.

'Perhaps, but it seemed more likely that he would try to prevent you from making contact with the farmer and thereby raising the alarm, and attending to me once you had been secured.'

By now we had reached the farmhouse where we found the owner, James Bowen and his wife, to be most affable and co-operative. A lad was dispatched to the village at once and Mrs Bowen afforded us a substantial tea which we had barely consumed by the time the local constabulary had arrived.

I was still harbouring certain misgivings over the manner in which Holmes had misused me in entrapping Tyler, although, his reaction upon finding me safe and well, had diluted these somewhat. However, his behaviour upon revealing the whereabouts of the stolen money to the local police was what surprised and gratified me the most. As he had calculated it was hidden in the fireplace of the middle cottage. Normally a situation such as this would provide him with a moment of supreme and dramatic triumph. As gratifying as this moment undoubtedly was, he accepted it with total nonchalance as he was clearly still distracted by the thought of the potential danger he had subjected me to.

The train journey back to London was both quiet and uneventful, but as I sat there in the carriage, observing how oblivious my friend was to the view from the window he was staring so intently through, I could not help surmising that the total dedication he afforded to his profession would not prevent him from using me in such a way once again, should the situation command it.

The Mystery of Avalon

During the months immediately following my marriage, I was totally immersed in setting up a home with my beloved Mary and establishing the small medical practice which had been neglected somewhat by my elderly predecessor, Dr Farquar.

The common indulgences of the Yuletide festivities, followed by a particularly cold early January, had led to a sharp, albeit temporary increase in the demands upon my services, the results of which had rendered me decidedly weary. Therefore, when a lull at last descended, around the tenth of the month, I confess to welcoming the opportunity to rest. The more so on this particular morning, for an overnight snowfall had continued into the morning, unabated, and I had spent much of the night tending at a patient's bedside.

Relaxing with my wife before a roaring fire after a hearty breakfast was the perfect remedy, so one could beg sympathy for my dismay at receiving an immediate summons from my old friend and colleague, Sherlock Holmes.

I examined the note with annoyance before hurling it into the fire. It read . . .

My Dear Watson. A most singular problem has been brought to my attention by a gentleman from Cornwall. Our client has just arrived, would be obliged by your immediate attendance. S.H.

P.S. My greetings to Mrs Watson.

'Our client indeed!' I protested. This use of the plural was strange for I had seen very little of Holmes over the past several months, and I had certainly missed the stimulation I had always gleaned from my humble involvement in his career.

The fault for this, however, was not mine alone, for while I had been preoccupied to the exclusion of my friend, it was equally true that he had not requested my assistance either. Apart, that is, from my brief involvement in the singular affair of the Blue Carbuncle. Nonetheless, there was no doubting the urgency of this problem, and I was intrigued to discover what should bring a client up from Cornwall during the depths of so harsh a winter.

'Your expression tells me that you feel you have to go,' my dear Mary astutely observed. 'Besides which, Doctor Jackson is able to take care of your patients, as well as his own, now that things have slackened off somewhat.'

I squeezed her hand appreciatively, and hastily prepared a bag for myself, while Mary arranged for a cab.

Despite my best intentions, my arrival at Baker Street was by no means an immediate one. The severe weather had rendered the task of procuring a cab a most difficult one, and once safely aboard I found the depth of the snow made our progress, even through the thoroughfares of central London, slow and sluggish.

Although it felt strange to see my old rooms again, Mrs Hudson's cheery greeting, and the sight of Holmes seated in his favourite chair, made me feel as if I had never been away.

Catching sight of my overnight bag, Holmes exclaimed, 'Dear friend Watson, prepared and reliable as ever, I see. Most good of you to attend so promptly, particularly since you were working through the night.'

Having observed my look of astonishment, he explained. 'Your shoes Watson, your shoes! Knowing too well the habits of a military man, the damp stains on your uppers indicate that they have been subjected to deep snow. Seeing that last night's fall did not commence until after midnight, and the paving on this side of Baker Street has been all but cleared, what other explanation can there be?' He spread out his hands as if he had just performed a conjuror's trick, and fell back into his chair.

'Now help yourself to the Persian slipper,' Holmes invited. 'While I introduce you to our esteemed visitor from Cornwall, Colonel Geraint Masterson. Colonel, my trusted friend and associate, Doctor Watson.'

Such was my pleasure, and relief, at finding things so delightfully unchanged in my old lodgings, that it was only now, as I stood by the fire replenishing my pipe, that I became aware of a third individual in the room. He was seated pensively, on the edge of the settee, directly across from Holmes.

For me to say that the Colonel's appearance and presence was startlingly impressive would be to understate in the extreme. Yet to define the cause of this effect was no easy task. His size certainly contributed to this. He stood at no less than six feet and two inches, but his military experience had given him an impressive build and bearing. I was equally taken aback by the manner in which he grew his hair and beard. Although, undoubtedly clean, and neatly cut, he had allowed the hair at the back of his head to grow to a level well below his shirt collar, indeed, it actually reached down to just above his shoulders. His beard, again, was neatly trimmed, yet was shaped to an unusual point, which reminded me of those paintings of medieval kings. His face was open and alert, while his smile was one that immediately inspired trust. A most singular individual indeed.

'Ah, Dr Watson!' he boomed. 'I, and the public at large, have you and your most excellent journals to thank for bringing to our attention the unique skills and talents of your colleague, Mr Holmes. For it is only he, I am sure, who is capable of lifting the dark cloud that at present hangs ominously over my household.'

Sherlock Holmes bowed his head in acknowledgement. 'It would render my task considerably easier if you could now furnish me with some facts,' he said sharply while lighting up his old clay pipe.

'Quite so, quite so, but where does one begin?' the Colonel pondered.

'I would strongly suggest at the beginning,' Holmes tersely observed, an attitude I found somewhat surprising considering the affable nature of the Colonel. Nevertheless, the Colonel mumbled apologetically, and I took out my notebook and pencil as he began his remarkable tale.

'Remember Colonel, omit nothing,'

Holmes added. 'That which you may consider trivial and inconsequential, may be the one missing piece of the puzzle whose absence might prohibit my success.'

The Colonel paused to reconsider his oration, and began his story.

'My family seat is a large, sprawling estate, near the village of Slaughter Bridge in the heart of Cornwall. No doubt because of the connection between the village, and the legendary last battle of King Arthur at Camlaan, my ancestors saw fit to name the house and the wild, rugged terrain that comprises our landholding, after the last resting place of Arthur, namely Avalon. As you might have gathered from my own first name, some of my ancestors took the idea of our Arthurian connection rather too seriously at times. Indeed my own name is not the first to appear in the family tree, that has been derived from the knights of the round-table. My father was named Percival, whilst my brother bore the name of Gareth.' Laughing nervously, the Colonel added, 'Our estate even contains a large mysterious lake, and we dine from a circular table.'

I could see from Holmes's vacant expression, that the significance of these Arthurian references had meant absolutely nothing to him and in confirmation of this he impatiently cajoled the Colonel to get to the point. He duly responded.

'Well, the plain and simple truth of the matter, Mr Holmes, is that someone is attempting to kill my dear wife, Alice. We have been married these past ten years, since I resigned my commission, in fact, and we have lived out these years, at Avalon, in absolute peace and harmony. Her love of Avalon is surely as deep as my own, and her kindly, and friendly manner, towards all of human kind, be he a rich, local landowner, or our lowliest servant, is universally reciprocated. Therefore, her current predicament is totally beyond all reason.'

'I assume,' Holmes began, leaning forward, his eyelids heavy in concentration, 'that this attempt on your wife's life was made recently?'

'Two,' the Colonel corrected. 'There

have been two murderous attacks upon her. This is why I could no longer tolerate the inadequacies of the local constabulary, and why I have made the long journey to London to seek your advice.'

Holmes waved aside this further compliment. 'The first attack occurred when precisely?'

'It was three days before Christmas and we had just completed our breakfast, when Alice decided to stroll down to the stables. As you may recall it was particularly cold at that time and she wished to ensure that our horses were being supplied with sufficient winter provisions. As she passed out of sight of the house and entered a small copse that lies between the house and the stables, she felt a huge hand reach out and grab her by the throat. She struggled for a moment, before a thick piece of cord replaced the hand and threatened to choke the life from her. She was fortunate in that she was carrying her heavy walking stick, which she used to lash out in all directions. The rope suddenly slackened and she heard her assailant run away into the trees. She saw no-one, Mr Holmes,' said a very solemn Colonel.

'Why, exactly, was your wife in need of a stick in the first place?' Holmes asked.

'Alice was still nursing an injury to her right leg that she sustained while out riding, some weeks previously.'

'I take it the police were called immediately after the attack and a thorough search made of the copse for traces of the assailant?' I asked, whilst noticing Holmes's look of surprised approval at my interjection.

'Indeed yes, but to no avail,' the Colonel replied. 'Not even a single footprint was visible. Unfortunately the heavy frosts had rendered the ground solid and hard.'

'Unfortunate indeed.' Holmes replied in a tone heavy with sarcasm, obviously already convinced of the ineptitude of the Cornish police. 'What, pray, were the exact circumstances of the second attack upon your wife?'

'As you might imagine, it was this further attempt upon my wife that prompted my journey to London. It took place yesterday morning and came considerably closer to succeeding than the first. In fact, my wife sustained some small injury to her right arm as a consequence. On this occasion the scoundrel used a crossbow, and fired while Alice was tending to her plants in our conservatory. The arrow came crashing through the glass and embedded itself in a wooden post attached to the far wall. Its trajectory caused it to skim Alice's arm and her profuse bleeding caused her to pass out for a few moments. I delayed my journey to London until I was certain of her recovery and that the police had taken all necessary steps.'

'I take it the enquiries of the police bore as little fruit as those on the previous occasion?' Holmes asked.

'Alas, that is true and yet, the unusual behaviour of our shepherd, of late, and his subsequent disappearance, seems to have drawn their attention and interest.'

'Ah . . . excellent!' Holmes exclaimed, suddenly sitting bolt upright, alert, and attentive. 'There are certain elements in your story that lift it above the mundane and routine. Indeed, Watson, I should not be surprised to see this tale take its place amongst your other, most vivid chronicles, one day. Initially, though, we must hear about this extraordinary shepherd.' Holmes said this while positively beaming with expectation.

Colonel Masterson swallowed hard before continuing, obviously taken aback by Holmes's outburst. Understandably, of course, as he did not know of Holmes's penchant for the more bizarre, and outlandish aspects of his investigations as well as I did.

'As you may know, gentlemen, the main body of Arthurian legend, though romantically embellished by twelfth century troubadours, is firmly rooted in the Dark Ages, the period immediately following the Roman withdrawal. In the minds of simple folk, and more especially during times of national crises, the hope remained that Arthur would rise again and wield Excalibur once more in the British cause. A further legend, perhaps of medieval origin, tells of a shepherd searching for a lost sheep on an isolated hilltop. During his search he stumbled across a hidden cave, finding within a huge treasure and King Arthur and his knights laid out in full armour. The awestruck shepherd decided to help himself to as much of the treasure as he could carry, and was on the point of departing, when Arthur suddenly awoke from his extended slumber. The king threatened to dismember the shepherd's head should he not replace the treasure, depart from the cave and swear an oath never to return. The terrified shepherd obviously complied immediately and the location of the cave has remained a mystery from that day to this.'

'Colonel, please!' Holmes impatiently interrupted. 'I will be more than willing to help identify your wife's would-be assailant, but please do not prevaricate with these tales of antique legends. They are of no use at all to a trained logician and I have no more interest in them than you have in the numerous varieties of cigar ash that I have studied over the years. Now please, stick to the facts!'

'To the minds of the simple local folk, I

include our wayward shepherd amongst these, these whimsical tales are as real as cigar ash!' The irony of these last words reflected the resentment Masterson felt to Holmes's attitude. 'However, the facts are these, Mr Holmes. On the very day of the crossbow attack, our shepherd was seen emerging from a concealed hole in a local hillside. He was then seen scurrying down its slippery, muddy slope. Mr Holmes, he has not been seen nor heard of since.' He concluded with a gruff finality and rose to his feet, obviously assuming that Holmes's interest, and involvement in the matter was surely at an end.

To our surprise, Holmes suddenly rose from his chair. 'A moment if you please, Colonel. Watson, I seem to remember there being a copy of Malory's *Le Morte d'Arthur*, amongst the volumes you have yet to transfer to your new nuptial abode. Would you please locate it for me?'

'Certainly, but I was under the impression you held no interest in such matters.' Without replying, Holmes gestured toward the bookshelves and I began my search.

'Colonel, I owe you a sincere apology. My friend Watson, here, will attest to my ignorance on certain subjects which is such that it leaves even him aghast at times. You see, I consider it wasteful to saturate the limited capacity of the human mind with information that is of no use to someone of my chosen profession. On this occasion, it seems, Arthurian legend warrants a place. I suggest you return to Cornwall, on the first available train, and maintain a vigil over your wife until Watson and I join you there tomorrow afternoon. Hopefully, my attic has sufficient temporary, capacity for Thomas Malory.'

It was left to me to show the befuddled Colonel to the door, for I had located my copy of Malory, and Holmes, his clay pipe already filled and alight, was now totally absorbed in its contents. Such was the depth of Holmes's concentration that I soon realized that any attempt at conversation or extracting an opinion from him on the subject of Masterson's wife, would prove to be futile. The arctic conditions precluded any notion I might have harboured of returning home for the night, so I spent the remainder of the day in a manner I had enjoyed on countless occasions, prior to my marriage, reading the papers by a cheery fire in the old room at Baker Street.

Mrs Hudson provided us with a simple, but ample supper, of which Holmes touched not a bit and at eleven o'clock I retired for the night to my old bedroom. I left Holmes with my Malory, in the aforementioned fashion, but had no idea as to what time he finally put it down.

I was greeted in the morning by the substantial volume hurtling towards my head, as I entered the sitting room.

'Watson! Be sure to catch your most excellent volume,' Holmes called to me.

'Steady on Holmes,' I protested, then added quizzically, once the book was safely in my hands. 'So it seems you enjoyed these whimsical stories.'

'They were certainly most entertaining.' He replied nonchalantly as he poured out some coffee. 'It was certainly interesting to note the various parallels to be drawn between your legendary King

Arthur and myself.'

'Parallels? With you? Surely not Holmes. I can see none,' I queried, assured of my friend's humorous intent.

'Oh yes Watson, there is not a doubt of it,' Holmes rejoined in surprising earnest. 'Consider, if you will for a moment, the significance of Arthur's holy realm of Logres. Throughout the land the old order of civilization was collapsing, and reverting to barbarism. The dark ages had fallen, and yet in the depths of this darkness shone a solitary light. A bright guiding light that was Arthur and his realm. The parallel is now obvious, when you consider the darkness that our regular police force is constantly stumbling around in. Not quite barbaric in method, perhaps, and yet their ignorance and ineptitude is tantamount to barbarism! Yet in their darkness shines a tiny light. The light of reasoning, logic, observation, and method. This small room and my humble practice is the modern, judicial realm of Logres and I, of course, the guiding light of Arthur.'

'Really Holmes!' I complained, annoyed

at this further example of my friend's arrogance and yet, somehow, amused, despite myself, at his presumptuousness.

'You must excuse my apparent vanity, Watson, yet it would be equally wrong should I belittle my efforts, and abilities. The devilled eggs look delicious, by the way,' he said, rising suddenly.

'Will you not join me?' I asked while taking my place at the table.

'Alas no. There are certain inquiries I must undertake before our departure from London. Our train leaves Paddington at 2.17, so I will meet you on the platform. I trust you have included your revolver amongst your luggage.' I nodded my affirmation as he hurried from the room.

Our train was true to its listing in Bradshaw and although I was pleased by my own punctuality, I found that Holmes was already settled in our carriage and enjoying his first pipe of the journey.

A half smile and a raised eyebrow in my direction were his only form of greeting, so I decided to keep to my corner of the carriage, buried in my *Telegraph*, until he was in a more communicative mood. There, almost lost within the middle pages, was a half column devoted to the attacks on the Colonel's wife. Though the article added little to our sparse knowledge, it drew some response from Holmes.

'Well done, Watson. It may be that an interview with that reporter may prove of more worth than anything we might learn from the police.'

'Have you formed no theory of your own yet, Holmes?' I asked.

'Watson, old friend, the Colonel has hardly furnished me with a surfeit of practical information. To theorise at this early stage, when our factual picture is predominately a void, would prove a fruitless waste of time. I assume that you have formulated a theory of your own,' he asked, turning his head from the window for the first time since our journey began.

Trying to conceal my surprise at his incredible intuition, I replied, 'It is not so much a theory, I suppose, and yet I find some of our scant information certainly suggestive. It seems fairly obvious to me that our mysterious shepherd is Alice Masterson's, thankfully, inept assailant. I can see no other reason for his sudden and bizarre disappearance.'

Holmes cast me a short, contemptuous glance. 'Considering his task remains incomplete, I would say his disappearance is all the more remarkable. No, Watson, I feel your solution is far from the truth. For a man to go to such lengths and take so great a risk to commit murder and then leave before achieving his goal, is beyond reason. Besides, there are very few shepherds for whom access to a crossbow is the norm.' He turned, dismissively back to the window, but then, perhaps aware of my crestfallen demeanour, he smiled briefly, and added, 'I am sure, however, that as our investigation progresses and more facts come to light, a significant link between this shepherd and our most singular problem, will be established.'

Content with that, at least, I returned to my paper, but I soon exhausted its articles of interest, and dozed off for an hour or more. When I awoke, I was immediately struck by the changes that had occurred to the landscape through which we were travelling. Warmer air was, evidently, blowing in from the west and the further we travelled in that direction, the more colourful the scenery became. Indeed, by the time we had reached our destination and were being jostled along to Avalon in an ancient trap, all traces of the snow had disappeared.

The desolate harshness of the Cornish landscape I was so used to in summer, was accentuated by the grey of winter and the gnarled barren trees. This setting seemed more than appropriate for the strange events about to unfold. The large, open lake we rode passed on our way to the house, was both serene and mysterious, shrouded, as it was, in a thin winter's mist. The main house itself was austere and imposing. The two wings flanked a wide gravel driveway and were separated by a huge, pillared staircase and entrance, all fashioned from the local, grey stone.

'I trust there will be sufficient elements of interest, in this case to warrant so infernal a journey!' Holmes complained as we pulled up outside the entrance to Avalon. Never at his happiest away from his beloved London, the chilliness of the air and the isolation of Avalon itself, made the whole excursion intolerable to him.

Our host was not on hand to receive us, but we were met by an elderly footman who raised his eyebrows quizzically, when he caught sight of Holmes's attempts at insulating himself. The large, heavy coat, the woollen blanket he held about him, and the enormous muffler.

'Mr Holmes?' he asked impressively, then after noting Holmes's half-hearted nod of affirmation, 'I have a message for you sir!' He announced handing Holmes a wire, one, presumably in answer to the inquiries he had made earlier in London. Holmes opened this at once, remaining in the trap while our luggage was being unloaded.

I alighted from the trap enthusiastically only to be held back by my friend's strange behaviour and appearance. It was almost as if the contents of the wire held him transfixed and he continued to stare at it as if he expected its contents to change suddenly. I returned to my seat in the trap and studied Holmes's peculiar transformation.

His eyes had lost their steely, grey sharpness and his lips their usual firmness of determination. His countenance had turned quite ashen, and his strong shoulders visibly drooped before my eyes. I even observed, I am sure, a slight, involuntary movement in the hand that held the cursed wire. When he eventually spoke his voice had lost its authority, and was no more than a hoarse whisper. I had to lean forward to render his words audible.

'We must return to London, on tomorrow morning's earliest available train. Watson, please make my apologies to the Colonel.' Then, addressing the footman, 'If my room is ready I shall go there at once, and remain there until our early morning departure. In the meantime, I shall require nothing.'

As can be imagined, I was mortified at seeing my friend reduced to this sorry state and surprised at hearing these strange pronouncements. As he descended from the trap, he denied me even the briefest of glimpses at the accursed wire and it was obvious that no explanation was to be forthcoming. His weak shamble, up the main stairs, was that of a stricken mourner. The footman shrugged his shoulders, seemingly as ignorant of the contents of the message as I surely was, he then instructed a lad as to the disposition of our luggage. While this was being attended to, a tall, distinguished butler led me through to the Colonel.

The drawing-room I was shown into was not the large, cold, stone chamber one would have expected. It was a spacious room certainly, yet the clever placing of comfortable furniture, and the warmth of the rich tapestries that adorned the walls, lent it an unexpected intimacy. The warmth from the huge fire further enhanced the comfort of the room, and the tapestries seemed to glow in its light. The Colonel, who had previously been leaning against the magnificent marble mantelpiece, whisky glass in hand, immediately sprang forward to greet me, pausing on his way to pour me a large measure of whisky from a fine crystal decanter.

'This will soon warm your chilled bones, Doctor Watson. Welcome to Avalon!' he boomed.

'I thank you for both. You have a fine home, Colonel,' I replied.

'I will show you around tomorrow and bore you with our Arthurian artefacts. Where is Mr Holmes?'

'Unfortunately, the harsh weather and the length of our journey have had an adverse effect upon his health. In fact, if you would excuse me I should go to examine him at once. At this stage I cannot be sure as to when he will be fit enough to commence his investigations.'

'Yes, yes: go to him and understand that my staff will be at your constant beck and call; anything you might require will be made available to you,' the Colonel offered. 'Please convey our wishes to Mr Holmes, for a speedy recovery.'

'Thank you Colonel, I will certainly inform him of your concern. I wonder how Mrs Masterson's arm is coming along. I shall be pleased to examine her wound if she is strong enough to join us later.'

'Join us!? Mrs Masterson!? Confound you, Doctor!' He bellowed these words like a maniac, and hurled his glass violently into the fireplace. Then he stormed out of the room, throwing furniture aside in his wake.

This sudden, irrational display of violent temper was inexplicable to me and I stood, for some moments, still holding my whisky, as one who is dumbstruck. I was certain that I had said nothing that could have been construed as offensive, indeed it had been Mrs Masterson's welfare that had prompted our journey to Cornwall. Therefore, there had to be another explanation for the Colonel's extraordinary behaviour and I hoped that Holmes's condition would improve sufficiently for him to be able to discover this.

The thought of having to locate the whereabouts of my room, in this grey stone labyrinth, was somewhat daunting, so I was relieved to find the footman still in close attendance when I turned to leave the drawing-room.

'Shall I show you to your room now, sir?' the elderly servant asked quietly. I could tell from his manner that, although he had been upset at Masterson's outburst, this had not been the first occasion he had witnessed such behaviour.

The room I was shown to was spacious and comfortable, though the cold stone walls made me glad of the roaring fire. I decided to waste no time in unpacking my bag, and went directly to the room opposite my own to inquire as to Holmes's current condition.

Upon receiving no response to my firm knock on his door, I entered the room quietly to find that he had not taken to his bed at all. Instead he was seated by a window that looked out over the front drive, in a high-backed chair, facing away from the door. He did not turn when I entered the room, therefore, it was only when I joined him at the window that I realized how unwell he really looked.

'Confound it, Holmes! You really must take to your bed and allow me to examine you.'

‘Please do not alarm yourself on my account, Doctor,’ Holmes whispered without turning toward me. ‘My condition has now greatly improved.’

‘There are no visible medical improvements that I can see. Your face is still pale and drawn, your eyes sunken and red. Although your condition might be put down to the weather and the journey, I know enough of your methods to realize that it has certainly been compounded by that wire,’ I replied anxiously.

‘Therefore, I am sure you feel entitled to know the exact contents of this communication,’ Holmes suggested, while turning towards me slowly.

‘If I am to be of assistance in clearing up this matter, I feel it is necessary,’ I replied.

‘Unfortunately this information is not mine to divulge and, equally, its very nature precludes us from taking any further interest in this matter and makes any action an impossibility. I think, perhaps, I am best left to my own company for the time being,’ Holmes suggested, smiling briefly, and enigmatically.

Reluctantly I agreed. 'Perhaps after some rest, and once the effect of the journey, and the contents of the wire have worn off, your judgement will return, and your decision alter.'

'Oh Watson!' he cried out, raising his right arm above his head in agitation. Then he added quietly, 'Perhaps you are right. We shall see.' He returned his gaze to the window, and assuming this to be by way of my dismissal, I returned to my room, and proceeded to dress for dinner.

The Colonel and I dined alone and, although I thought it prudent not to enquire as to his wife's whereabouts, I found it most unusual that she chose not to join us. The dining room was as large and sumptuous as the drawing-room and I was amazed to discover that the Colonel's allusion to a round table was no jest. He sat on a tall throne-like carver and the Arthurian subject dominated our conversation. Any mention I might have made of his wife and the murderous attacks she had experienced, were met by polite rebuffs from my host, while his enquiries as to the state of Holmes's health, were met similarly by myself. No mention was made of his earlier violent display, and it seemed that none of these issues would be resolved until Holmes was fit and well once more.

Once we had partaken of an excellent meal, the Colonel led me back to the drawing-room where we enjoyed some fine cigars and an extremely old port. As the evening progressed, however, I became aware of my host's growing agitation. He continually withdrew his watch, which, on each occasion, he examined at some length, almost as if he expected the time to suddenly change. I excused myself at an early hour and decided to look in on Holmes before retiring for the night.

He was as I had left him, seated motionless before the window, yet when he turned towards me, I could see that some of his earlier agitation had been replaced with one of his dark moods.

'Have you been privileged enough to make the acquaintance of our charming hostess yet?' He asked with surprising sarcasm in his voice.

Whereupon I narrated to him the

strange interview I had experienced earlier with the Colonel and its most singular conclusion. I also voiced concern at his unusual behaviour during the course of the evening, with allusion to his constant time watching.

'I am afraid that the situation is very much as I suspected,' Holmes said while withdrawing his old clay pipe and a pouch of shag from his jacket pocket.

'Suspected!?' I queried excitedly. 'I was under the impression that you had formulated no theory on the subject, due to sparse information.'

Holmes sat smoking in silence for a moment or two, while he was, no doubt, reaching his decision as to whether to confide in me or not. He obviously reached an affirmative decision, for he turned his chair around and motioned for me to assume the chair opposite his own.

'My suspicions were born simply by possessing prior knowledge and experience of the character, and behaviour of Alice Dunwoody.'

Though I am somewhat ashamed to admit it, for a moment I suspected that a fever, or the shock he had received in the wire, had somehow damaged Holmes's wonderful mind.

'Oh Watson, you look so bemused! Surely I am referring to the maiden name of the Colonel's wife. The very information I have received in that infernal wire.'

'Yet why should that information have had such a profound effect upon you? Besides, what prior knowledge could you possibly have of Mrs Masterson's character and behaviour?' I asked.

Holmes smoked again, before continuing. 'On more than one occasion, within your most excellent, yet over-dramatised journals, you have referred your readers to my machine-like exclusion of all emotion and feeling. Repeatedly you have expressed surprise at my abhorrence of emotional expression and romance and my disregard of any praiseworthy qualities the female of our species might possess. Save, of course 'The Woman' Irene Adler and even in her case, as you correctly pointed out, my interest was of a more professional leaning.

'I assure you, Watson, that had I been

in your place, upon being confronted with such a singular trait in an acquaintance, I would have used my method to unravel the chain of events that might have resulted in such a characteristic. Perhaps it has not occurred to you that this supposed abhorrence of both female kind and the idea of close attachment, is nothing less than a fear of the same.'

'No, Holmes,' I admitted. 'In all honesty, I cannot say that it has.'

'Well, friend Watson, although it shames me to admit to such a thing, that is the truth of the matter.'

I emitted a long whistle, and sank back in my chair in disbelief. I studied Holmes, in a moment of contemplation and realized that, since we had started this conversation, his nerve had become steadier than before and his voice stronger, he was surely telling me the truth. My surprise at this revelation can be well understood, under the circumstances. From the day of our very first meeting and up to the moment of Holmes's revelation that he had a brother, I was under the illusion that

Holmes was unlike other men. No family, no friends, no romantic attachments, in fact the sublime professional. An emotionless, dedicated, logical pure mind in human guise. Mycroft's existence was a disillusioning revelation in itself, but this!

'This woman has, clearly, caused you considerable pain,' I announced solemnly.

'It is not a subject on which I wish to dwell; indeed I only mention it now because of its relevance to the problem on which we are now engaged. Suffice it to say that bitter experience has shown to me the depraved nature of this woman's character. She has reinvented the meaning of the words; *deceitful*, and *promiscuous* and her guile and charms would have subjugated stronger men than Masterson and myself.'

'My dear fellow, I had no idea. I quite understand and agree with your decision to return to London forthwith, as, I am sure will our client,' I replied.

At this Holmes became quite agitated. He stood up, suddenly, and began pacing the room.

'Watson, understand me well. Under

no circumstances can the Colonel learn the truth about my prior involvement with his wife. This would surely jeopardise any chance we may have of success in this matter. Now I must rest, for I will require all my physical resources for the day's work ahead.'

I got up, and walked to the door.

'I take it we shall not be returning to London in the morning,' I asked, turning back. In the time it had taken me to walk to the door and turn around, Holmes had lain himself on the bed, fully clothed and on his back, already in deep slumber. This, I felt, boded ill for any foe that Holmes had set his mind on hunting down.

Having left Holmes in such a state of exhaustion, I was more than a little surprised to discover that he was up, had breakfasted and gone out, a full half hour before I had even reached the dining-room the following morning. It was not unusual for Holmes to go about his work without consulting me beforehand, but on this occasion I was clueless as to what direction his inquiries were to take. I took my breakfast alone, for word came to me that the Colonel was indisposed, and had decided to keep to his room. Any inquiries I made of the staff, as to the nature of his illness, or to the whereabouts of his wife, were met with a stony silence.

I took the papers into the drawing-room with my pipe and was resolved to spending the morning exploring the estate alone, when Holmes suddenly burst in upon me. The old, familiar gleam of excitement was in his eyes once more, and I knew he had discovered some clue.

'Ah, Watson, I see that you have finally decided to emerge from your bed,' was his jovial greeting. 'You will be glad to hear that I have succeeded in locating your legendary cave of King Arthur, and I am certain that the Colonel can help us identify its contents!'

Whereupon I explained to him what little I knew about the Colonel's illness. Yet, undaunted, Holmes hastily scratched out a brief note, and dispatched this to the Colonel's room by way of a pageboy. Not sharing Holmes's confidence, I was most surprised when, after little more than ten minutes had passed, Colonel Masterson shuffled into the room, betraying every sign of being a broken man.

'I was a fool in attempting to outwit the illustrious Sherlock Holmes,' the Colonel mumbled apologetically.

This compliment was not lost on my friend, who, with a dramatic flourish, waved the Colonel to one of his own chairs. Holmes, in turn, took up a position by the fireplace, whilst lighting his pipe. A glance from Holmes prompted me to take out my notebook, and pencil.

'Even the sparse contents of your note have shown to me the futility of any further deception on my part,' the Colonel stated. 'However, I am at a loss to understand how a single morning's investigation could have revealed so much to you. What glaring error have I committed?'

'You have allowed pride to cloud your reason,' Holmes replied. 'Why else should you go to such lengths in concealing your wife's infamous behaviour? I can assure you that I have performed no miracle.

Such indiscretions, as perpetrated by your wife, can not go long unnoticed in so small a community, I assure you. The few inquiries that I made this morning have shown me how affairs really stand. Yet these discoveries alone would have proved nothing, in themselves, save only your wife's lack of scruples. However a small hoard of treasure, removed from your own home, that I discovered in the, supposed, cave of King Arthur, indicate to me that her affair with the shepherd has progressed further, and deeper than any on which she has previously embarked. The haul in the cave was intended to have been their nest-egg and their means to flight. So determined were you not to be revealed as a cuckold to this shepherd that even this violation was left unreported to the police. For only then would it have been seen that your wife was not the victim, in fear of her life, acting under coercion, but a more than willing accomplice.'

'Mr Holmes you have described my predicament with remarkable clarity, and, I might add, with a deep insight and understanding,' the Colonel responded.

I could see Holmes becoming increasingly agitated at these words, no doubt concerned that the genuine reasons for his understanding might now become clearer to the Colonel. To ease his discomfiture, I made my own contribution.

'Colonel, my own experience of the fairer sex has shown that you are not the first, nor will you be the last, to succumb to the wiles of such a woman. They are driven along their treacherous path by something from within and her behaviour reflects on you not at all.'

He bowed in acknowledgement, and then asked, 'Mr Holmes, you have failed to explain how you were so successful in locating this cave, whereas the regular police force, with their superior numbers, failed so abjectly.'

'It was not I who located the cave,' Holmes replied.

'Oh, come along Holmes! You just said . . .' Holmes would not allow me to complete my protest.

'Watson, surely you remember our investigation of the most singular problem posed by the Sign of Four?' Then upon noting my nodded affirmation, 'Well, then you will also doubtless recall the more than significant contribution made by our canine friend, Toby. I simply put that method to use once more. In my experience, there is no more loyal or perceptive a beast than the sheep dog, and so it proved. I merely removed a well worn boot from the shepherd's lodge, and presented this to the animal's nose. In consequence it was he who presented me with the cave.'

'Holmes,' I then inquired. 'This is all very well, but surely this new information, as to the true nature of Mrs Masterson's amour, clouds still further the central issue of who perpetrated the murderous attacks upon her?'

'Watson I see that, even now, you still cling to your original hypothesis regarding the shepherd. It is now patently obvious. There have been no attacks made upon the life of Mrs Masterson, merely attempts to make it appear as if there had been. How else could the Colonel incriminate the shepherd, and hope to win back his wife? By seeking my assistance, he intended to confirm, and consolidate the case for the slow-moving police,' Holmes replied.

'Surely you are merely making an assumption on this point? The police could not discover a single clue at the scene of either attack. Therefore, even if the attacks were not genuine, the identity of the attacker must remain a mystery.' Even as I spoke, I immediately regretted my use of the word 'assumption'.

Holmes turned on me at once and with venom. 'I never guess . . . or assume, Watson! Whilst it is true to say that no clues were to be found at the scene of the first attack, there was certainly some information to be gleaned outside the conservatory.' He paused for a moment, to draw long and hard on his pipe.

'I do not understand, Mr Holmes,' the Colonel began, taking advantage of the momentary lull. 'The police drew a line that corresponded to the trajectory of the arrow, and searched the ground most thoroughly along that line until they were out of range. They were unsuccessful in finding a mark, or print of any description.'

'Ah, but Colonel, that is exactly what made me suspicious!' Holmes surveyed the bewildered looks on both our faces, and evidently drew some amusement from the sight. 'There should have been some footprints there, for they showed quite clearly immediately outside the conservatory door. The route, back to the house, crosses the line along which the arrow was fired. Therefore, someone had gone to great pains to obliterate those prints. The same person, of course, who had removed the crossbow from your armoury, Colonel.'

'You are certain the bow came from there?' Masterson asked.

'Naturally. A quick examination, this morning, revealed a thin layer of dust on all of the weapons, save for one crossbow! I was now certain that you were the supposed attacker and yet I was equally assured of your lack of genuine malicious intent, save, of course the incrimination of your rival. Even if one allows for your being a poor archer, I am sure a stick, wielded by a woman, would prove a most inadequate weapon when used against a man of your build and strength.'

'You have laid my secret bare most thoroughly, Mr Holmes, and your considerable reputation is certainly not mere hyperbole. However, I fail to see what steps you intend to take against me, since no crime, of which I am aware, has actually been committed. John Rouse, the shepherd is still at liberty, and my wife is free to go her own way, despite my own misgivings on the matter.' Masterson made this last statement with a curious mixture of defiance, and intense bitterness in his voice. This was not lost on Holmes, who replied with some sympathy.

'Even if I were able, I am sure I would take no action that would actually affect your liberty. Though not uncommon, your loss is great enough. When Watson and I finally depart for London, I can assure you, we will be leaving the Cornish police none the wiser.'

With a sigh of relief and not without some difficulty, the Colonel raised himself from his chair, and then proceeded to pour us each a large measure of whisky. The eagerness with which Holmes accepted his glass was a further indication of the intense strain he had been under, these past twenty-four hours. I further conjectured as to the course his investigation might have taken had he not his own bitter experience of the behaviour of the former Alice Dunwoody to draw upon.

'Mr Holmes, before you make your departure, there is one last favour I must ask of you.' My surprise at these words from the Colonel broke my chain of thought. 'You must help me to locate my wife, so I can yet persuade her to return to Avalon with me.' Sensing our astonishment, at this request, he added. 'Despite her wanton behaviour, I regret to say that I am still very much in love. Despite the humiliation she has brought on me, I am willing to forgive her, as Arthur forgave Guinevere. Will you help me?'

We stared at Holmes as he pondered over his decision. He sat in distracted silence, no doubt recalling his own feelings at the time when his association with Alice Dunwoody reached this very juncture.

'Is there a quiet, discreet hotel in Slaughter Bridge, or thereabouts?' Holmes asked thoughtfully.

'Only 'The Mitre Inn' immediately springs to mind,' the Colonel replied, after a moment's thought.

'Excellent!' Holmes responded, evidently having decided to help the Colonel this one last time. 'I suggest we begin our search there. Since the proceeds of their pilfering still remain within the cave, I am certain they will be using local accommodation. Watson and I shall pack at once, and meet you at the front in five minutes. If my surmise proves correct, we shall go directly from 'The Mitre' to the station in plenty of time to meet the London train.'

Within five minutes of Holmes's pronouncement, we found ourselves being driven away from the mysterious house of Avalon, although our return journey was to be made within the comfort of the Colonel's Landau, as opposed to the antique trap we had used the day before. Our journey was made in total silence, each of us harbouring his own thoughts. Holmes was seated next to the Colonel, and from my vantage point opposite, I was struck by the contrast in their nature and behaviour.

Holmes's normally, stony countenance was at its most impassive and enigmatic, and he was seated bolt upright as motionless as a statue, staring straight before him. The Colonel, however, was the epitome of restless agitation, constantly tugging at his high collar, or pulling at his tie. His legs, and feet were constantly in motion, as he persistently crossed and recrossed them. His forehead was locked in a perpetual scowl, and, despite the exceedingly low temperatures, I observed tiny beads of perspiration forming around the rim of his hat.

The outcome of the projected meeting was impossible to foresee, so I contented myself by surveying the most striking landscape we were passing through, once I was certain that there was to be no conversation forthcoming from my companions.

'The Mitre Inn' was located on the very

edge of the village and had the air of being seldom used. Being built of the local stone, it appeared to be well maintained however, and I was sure it had been standing in this fashion for hundreds of years, providing discreet comfort for the weary traveller.

Claiming fatigue, Holmes declined to leave the landau, and entreated me to accompany the Colonel, to ensure that the proposed liaison went well. I fully understood the reason behind Holmes's deception, and immediately alighted with the Colonel. Our initial inquiries of the inn's dusty reception clerk, had been fruitless, and I was despairing of meeting with any success, when the Colonel let out a short, startled cry.

I followed his gaze down the corridor, and standing there, was perhaps, the most strikingly beautiful woman I had ever beheld. Perhaps a shade too thin of build for total perfection, she stood well above average height, and held herself with a regal dignity that was awe-inspiring to watch. Her hair was ebony black, and shone with a wondrous lustre. Unfortunately, I was not able to distinguish her features initially, for she halted at the base of the stairs, evidently waiting for someone to join her. When her companion eventually arrived, they strode purposefully, almost defiantly, towards the Colonel and me, and I was then able to see that her features were nature's own gift. Her clear, dark eyes shone, her nose was small, and perfectly formed, whilst her fine, high cheek bones lent something imposing to her beauty. The effect she undoubtedly had on Holmes and the many who had since followed and succumbed, was not hard to believe now that I was in her presence.

Despite his attire, her companion, undoubtedly John Rouse, had an open, honest face, baring the ruddiness of a man who spends the majority of his time out of doors. A squarely built man in his early forties, Rouse exuded the impression of strength, and held himself well. Yet, even with these virtues, he seemed the unlikeliest of companions for the delightful creature by his side. I could well understand the Colonel's chagrin at her desertion to this man.

With an inconceivable air of confidence and lack of remorse, Alice Masterson approached her husband and greeted us both in a light, almost melodic voice. I introduced myself with a short bow, yet even as I spoke the Colonel moved a step forward and grabbed his wife by the arm.

'Please Alice,' he implored. 'Spare me just five minutes, so that we may speak alone. In there perhaps.' He motioned towards a deserted lounge that opened on to the lobby.

'Now see here Alice,' Rouse protested, then gesturing towards me. 'This here gentleman may well be to do with the police. Let us give back the silver and be gone from these parts, before any real harm is done.'

'You Sir!' Masterson boomed at Rouse, emphasising his physical superiority as he did so. 'Have already done very considerable harm, but my business here is with my wife!' Then calming himself, not wishing to create a public scene, 'I assure you that if I fail to convince her of the sincerity of my forgiveness and she chooses to remain here, I will return, in peace, to Avalon. As far as I am concerned, the silver can rot in the cave forever.'

Rouse was about to protest still further, but Alice Masterson merely squeezed his arm and assured him that all would be well. The door to the lounge was made up of glass panels, enabling Rouse, and myself to see the Mastersons clearly during the course of their conversation. However they chose to stand at the far end of the lounge and their words were lost to us. She was facing the door, while they spoke, and the Colonel kept his back to us.

Not surprisingly this conversation was in some earnest, and with emotion, yet both displayed commendable restraint and no loss of temper was evident. Rouse became agitated, when the couple fell into an embrace. I had to restrain him, though mercifully, without the use of force from entering the room there and then. I was wondering whether this embrace indicated their reconciliation, when Alice Masterson suddenly jerked backwards.

Initially, the significance of this was lost on us, as we watched from the lobby, however, a moment later she began to fall to the ground. In vain she tried to hold on to the Colonel for support, while he, in turn, stood rigid, as if transfixed, or in a trance. She landed heavily on the floor and at once we could see the dagger in her midriff and a large circle of scarlet forming around it.

'For heaven's sake!' Rouse screamed as he rushed to the door. Again, I was fortunate in being able to restrain him, for he would surely have killed the Colonel had I not held him back. I persuaded him to fetch the police at once, for fear of the Colonel escaping, although in fact I felt this most unlikely. However Rouse's departure averted another tragedy and, once he was safely away, I was able to enter the lounge, and attend to Mrs Masterson's wounds. Tragically, this was futile. She had died instantaneously, so violent, and accurate had been her husband's thrust with the knife. I turned my attention towards the Colonel.

As I had feared, he appeared to have

been taken by an attack of brain fever. His mouth was moving endlessly, though the sounds that he made were unintelligible. His eyes were fixed in a ghastly stare, and his limbs were still rigid with a small quantity of blood on his left hand, dripping slowly from it onto the pale rug. The perspiration on his face, and forehead was profuse, indicating to me that the murder of his wife had been premeditated. Surely the perspiration I had noticed on him, during our ill-fated journey to the inn, had been in anticipation of his dreadful crime.

Mercifully the police were most prompt in their arrival. The body of that beautiful creature was borne respectfully away and a police doctor attended to the Colonel, before much time had passed. It only remained for me to give my statement to the inspector, certain in the knowledge that each word I spoke was condemning the man to the gallows. It was only then that I was able to rejoin my friend in the carriage outside.

I must confess to being most surprised at finding him still seated there. I was certain that the commotion caused by the arrival of the police entourage would have attracted his attention to the inn. Even when I recounted the tragic outcome of the meeting inside, I was dismayed to observe not the faintest flicker of surprise or regret register on his stony countenance.

I was forced to reflect on how often, in the past, Holmes had acted as judge and jury, meeting out his own idea of justice, and not always in a manner of which I had approved. Yet in my heart of hearts I could not bring myself to believe that he had any prior knowledge, or suspicion of Masterson's dark intent.

To admit that would be to acknowledge that Holmes had decided, himself, the form of punishment that Alice Masterson's previous crimes were to receive. That notion, I decided, was inconceivable. It was far more likely that Holmes was now completely emotionally drained and that he had retreated, once more, into his shell. Indeed, never again was I to receive such an insight into his true nature and we regarded the subject as a closed book for the remainder of our association.

'The local police can conclude the little that still remains to be done,' Holmes said at last. 'At least that much can be entrusted to them,' he added disdainfully.

'Holmes,' I asked quietly. 'Surely you will go inside for a moment.'

'What, and miss our train? To the station, driver!'

The Missing Don Giovanni

'You know, Watson,' Holmes began one morning whilst casting his newspaper to the floor, 'if this continues for too much longer, I shall seriously have to consider changing my profession. To say there is a dearth of noteworthy crimes at the moment, would be to commit an understatement of unprecedented proportions.'

'It must be the heat,' I ventured, 'after all it has led to changes in everyone's behaviour.'

'I am not conscious of any noteworthy changes in my own,' Holmes replied, 'save the normal seasonal change of weight in my clothes. I shall leave the masses to wail and moan over nothing more than a few extra degrees.'

'A few extra degrees! Come now Holmes, it has been in the nineties since early June.'

I left our breakfast table hurriedly and went for a wash and change of clothes, a pattern that had become regular and tedious since the onset of this abnormal weather. Both the heat and Holmes's superior attitude had started to annoy me. Normally the heat causes me few problems, but the humidity of a large city made it unbearable, even with my experience of Afghanistan.

After I had washed and changed and was feeling considerably cooler, I reflected that, perhaps, my annoyance had been somewhat misplaced. The earlier superciliousness of Holmes was one of many stark changes of mood I had noticed come over him of late. Languid lethargy one moment, nervous, almost quirky excitement the next. Deep depression, followed by great exaltation expressed at mere trivia, for nothing other than trivia had occupied our time of late.

Therein, I was certain, lay the problem. Total inactivity of a professional nature was preventing the incredible mental powers of Sherlock Holmes from expressing themselves.

Then an even darker thought crossed my troubled mind. Was his dormant habit of cocaine taking, raising its ugly head again? I had been witness to the terrible effects of this awful drug on many occasions during periods of inactivity, but always, thankfully, a new intrigue or adventure would present itself, and his need for stimulation would evaporate.

It was true to say that this was the longest lull we had so far experienced. However, it was with foreboding that I conjectured on the long-term effects the drug might now be having.

I decided, therefore, that to remain in our rooms any longer would be dangerous to us both and to my pleasant surprise, succeeded in persuading Holmes to take a constitutional with me to clear our heads.

I immediately noticed how slowly the normal traffic and bustle of Baker Street was moving. Evidently the intense heat was affecting every walk of life, though when I mentioned this to him, Holmes merely waved my remark aside impatiently and trotted off at a deliberately brisk pace towards Marylebone Road.

We had gone no further than twenty yards when the clear tones of Mrs Hudson calling our names brought us to an abrupt halt. We turned sharply in our tracks and noticed a smart brougham drawn up outside our rooms and two equally well turned-out gentlemen standing with Mrs Hudson, evidently the vehicle's former occupants. The most striking feature of the two gentlemen, obvious, even at that distance, was that they were both attired in evening wear.

'Gracious Holmes, evening suits, mid morning and in this heat?'

'Evidently, Watson, some tragedy has befallen the Royal Opera House, Covent Garden.'

Before I could even begin to question this startling statement of his, Holmes was retracing his steps in great haste.

Despite the absence of dampness or cold, my leg had been playing me up of late, so by the time I was able to reach our rooms, our two guests were already seated opposite Holmes, who was in his customary chair. Impatiently he motioned me to mine, which I readily took, notebook at the ready.

'Watson, may I introduce Sir James Mowbray, director of the Royal Opera House, Covent Garden and his assistant, Mr Jonathan Crawford. Gentlemen, my good friend and staunch ally, Dr John Watson, whose discretion you can rely upon as readily as my own.

'Sir James, I can see from your attire that the problem which has brought you here has kept you up all night. I take it the police have been called, but have proved to be of no assistance at this stage. Therefore, an acquaintance of yours, who has either benefited from my services at some time or heard of such an instance, suggested you consult me. That much is clear. The remainder, I shall trust to your brief summary, for I am sure that time is at a premium!'

'Most impressive, Mr Holmes. You were quite correct on all counts and our time is indeed at a premium. The case, as the police and no doubt yourselves call it, which I bring before you is straightforward enough in itself, a missing person. The person in question, however, and the nature of his disappearance, are the conundrums. If either of you have any knowledge of, or interest in, serious music and more specifically grand opera, you will no doubt be aware of the Royal Opera's current production of Mozart's masterpiece, 'Don Giovanni'.'

'Why yes, of course and you brought over a supposedly wonderful young Italian baritone for the lead role. His name, however, escapes me,' I finished weakly.

'Roberto Tordelli, to be precise, doctor, and believe me, the reputation that preceded him was not unfounded. He has, without doubt, one of the finest voices for his age that I have been privileged to hear. In fact I might say, as fine a baritone as I have heard at any age, he is, after all, only twenty-four. A natural clear voice unforced and combined with instinctive interpretation.'

Sir James fell into a peculiar trance as he thought of the young Italian baritone, until Holmes brought him back to the business at hand.

'Sir James, please! If I am to be of any

assistance to you, you must give me the facts, precisely and briefly. I take it the young Tordelli is the aforementioned missing person?'

'I apologise, Mr Holmes, but the arrival in the opera world of such a talent is so rare an occurrence that to lose him so suddenly is a bitter blow.'

'I am sure also, that the loss of advance bookings, following so triumphant a first night, must weigh heavily with you as well. That is neither here nor there. However, I must inform you at once gentlemen, that missing persons are not the type of work that I would normally like to undertake. I am sure so illustrious a person as yourself will exact the maximum effort from our beloved police force.'

With that Holmes took up his pipe and turned to the window, his back to Sir James.

'Well, I must say!' Sir James protested. I merely shrugged by way of an apology. It was obvious that something in Sir James's manner had irritated Holmes's already lacerated nerves. There was no other explanation for his dismissal of our dignified visitors as he had been so desperate for a case of this level to come into our hands.

'Perhaps, even if you have no sympathy for my plight, Mr Holmes, you would consider Tordelli's charming young fiancée who arrived in London just hours after Tordelli's disappearance,' Sir James ventured.

Holmes smoked for a few moments in silence, his eyes still on Baker Street.

'Unannounced?' He asked quietly, without turning round.

'Why no. We received a telegram informing us of her intentions yesterday morning.'

Slowly Holmes turned. 'A point of most singular interest, would you not say, Watson?'

I nodded my agreement as Holmes resumed his seat.

'Tell me, Sir James, when did you first hear of this Italian protégé?'

Still suppressing his indignation, Sir James replied. 'About three months ago, two members of our committee heard him perform Verdi's 'Tosca' at La Scala in Milan. Acting on their ardent advice we immediately set in motion arrangements for his season here, as soon as his Italian commitments had been made good.'

'Unseen and unheard, quite an expensive gamble, I should imagine.' Holmes conjectured.

'Expensive, yes, as to a gamble, I assure you that the judgement of our committee members is both proven and unbiased,' Sir James replied pompously.

'Unbiased? A curious word in this instance,' Holmes spoke quietly, almost to himself.

'A singer's manager or family will go to great lengths to further the careers of their charge. It was not unheard of, in the past, for our agents to accept bribes, or to be otherwise seduced and influenced in their judgements and recommendations. I, however, have been most selective in my choice of agents and have not, so far, been disappointed. Indeed, even now the two in question are on their way, to a festival in Bavaria to judge the performances of another prospective singer.'

‘I am sure your confidence is well founded, but I must confess to being surprised at their not attending the young Tordelli’s first night, here at Covent Garden. However, please tell me how he was met at Victoria and his exact schedule since then.’

This time Crawford answered. ‘I met him off the boat-train last Friday evening and we went straight to his hotel where I stayed with him until I was sure his needs had been fully accommodated and that he was settled for the night. The next morning I collected him at an early hour for rehearsals which he attended most diligently throughout the day. Unfortunately we were working to a tight schedule. You see, originally, weeks of rehearsal were planned before his opening night, but his predecessor was taken ill and he had to step in at the last moment. Therefore, Sunday was the second and last day of rehearsal and he made his debut the night before last. During the weekend he was either at rehearsal or his hotel in my company. Indeed after his great triumph on Monday, we repeated our routine of an early night at his hotel. That, too, would have been our procedure tonight, but for his untimely disappearance.'

'Ah yes!' rejoined Holmes. 'Now to the crux of the matter. It was usual, I take it, for performers to return to their dressing rooms unattended after a performance?'

'For a few moments, at least,' Crawford replied, 'to change and regain some composure. Then, close friends, family and occasionally members of the reputable press are admitted to offer congratulations and the like. In the case of Tordelli, however, it was to be restricted to only Sir James, myself and the critic from the *Times*. We allowed him ten minutes before arriving at his room, by which time . . . '

'Ah, yes, of course he had disappeared,' Holmes interrupted curtly. 'Did the police detect any signs of a struggle?'

'None at all. The room was in perfect order apart from his costume strewn hurriedly across the floor.'

'I take it the stage door is usually attended?' Holmes asked.

'Yes of course, we cannot have just

anyone wandering in from the street causing a nuisance. A uniformed steward is always in attendance.' Sir James answered sharply, obviously still smarting from Holmes's earlier rebuttal.

'Did the police interview this individual?'

'Yes, but I am afraid he had nothing illuminating to impart.'

'That remains to be seen. Very well, gentlemen!' Holmes exclaimed. 'I think a visit to the young Tordelli's dressing room may prove of interest and since there is no time to lose I prevail upon you, Watson, to summon a hansom in all haste.' With that he jumped up and held open the door for our clients.

The cab journey to Covent Garden, though not long in distance, seemed almost interminable, hindered, as we were, by the heavy, slow moving London traffic. Our clients and I became hot and most agitated, perspiring profusely, while, in contrast Holmes appeared cool and impassive, forever staring out of the window, but seeing, I perceived, nothing whatsoever of his surroundings. Already his immense capacity for concentration was employed on the mystery of Tordelli and his whereabouts.

It was with immense relief that we alighted from our sweat-box of a cab and Sir James immediately led us to the rear of the Opera House and through the stage-door entrance. We followed him along narrow, dimly lit corridors until I became aware that Holmes was no longer with us. With Crawford's guidance, I retraced my steps and found Holmes engaged in conversation with a smart young fellow, obviously in attendance at the stage-door, who, I must confess, I had failed to notice when we entered the building. Holmes, of course, missed nothing.

As he came to join us, I shot him a questioning glance, but this he offhandedly waved aside as he hurried to join Sir James. A glimmer of a smirk played on his lips and already, I knew, Holmes was one step ahead of the rest of us.

The dressing room was surprisingly small and cramped, with no trace of the glamour one might have expected. A huge mirror surrounded by lamps, obviously to assist in the application of make-up, filled the wall facing the door. An immense wardrobe and a dressing screen were the room's only other features of interest, apart, that is, from some of Tordelli's costume strewn in the middle of the floor.

A quick examination of the wardrobe appeared to reveal nothing, so Holmes turned his attention to the clothes on the floor. He picked up every item, slowly examining each one in turn. I heard him mumble the words, 'strange' and 'unusual' to himself a couple of times and he turned the clothes over in his hands, oblivious to Sir James's undisguised impatience.

'Sir James, I take it these clothes were tailored to exact measurements?'

'No expense is spared at the Royal Opera, Mr Holmes. Our agents wired the measurements from Italy and they were immediately forwarded to one of the finest bespoke tailors in Savile Row,' Sir James replied.

'Mr Crawford, you can furnish me with

the name and address of the tailors, no doubt.'

'Of course, but why it should be relevant I fail to see.'

'The relevance, admittedly, has yet to be proved, but nevertheless . . . In the meantime, however, I should be grateful if you would accompany Doctor Watson and myself to Tordelli's hotel suite. There is nothing more to be learnt here.' Holmes said this with obvious disappointment, but as we turned to leave I noticed him paying close attention to a small, empty ashtray on the edge of the dressing-table.

Mercifully, the drive to Tordelli's hotel was a short one and we soon found ourselves at one of those small, comfortable and elegant gentleman's hotels with which London abounds. Parquet flooring, dark relaxing colours, subdued lighting, all added to the impression of a club, with accommodation. Crawford had chosen well, for the hotel was ideally suited for a young gentleman seeking solitude, quiet and unobtrusive service.

A smart, young under-manager greeted

us. He proved only too glad to co-operate provided it expedited the departure of the nuisance our investigation represented to him. Tordelli's suite was on the first floor and we were assured it had remained untouched since the morning of his last departure.

The suite was not particularly well appointed and although the décor was in good order, the furniture was old and worn, despite its undoubted quality.

Disdainfully Holmes observed, 'I see the bed has been made up, and the room cleaned, and tidied, rendering my search for clues a complete waste of time!'

'Naturally, Mr Holmes. Since Mr Tordelli's disappearance was in the evening, the maid was merely carrying out her routine morning duties.'

'Quite so.' Holmes grunted as he began his search of the wardrobe. A few moments of rummaging through the clothes seemed to satisfy him and then he turned suddenly, 'I should like to interview this maid, if she is on duty,' he announced.

'Certainly, Mr Holmes, I believe she is

cleaning the rooms on the second floor.' The under-manager replied.

'Excellent! I shall meet you all in the lobby in five minutes.' He said speeding from the room and rushing up the stairs, leaving us all as bemused as before.

Once again I found myself shut out of Holmes's innermost thoughts, my feelings apparently weighing as lightly in his mind as those of our clients or the other observers. My grasp of the case was as inadequate as theirs and Holmes obviously had no intention of enlightening me, even to a small degree. Feeling somewhat put-out and hurt, I left the others waiting in the stuffiness of the lobby and smoked in the relative coolness of the street outside.

So consumed was Holmes by his current problem, that all lethargy had been cast aside. His energy now knew no bounds and he was racing down the hotel stairs before I had even finished my cigarette.

In no time at all another hansom was conveying us back to Covent Garden to deposit Mr Crawford.

Before alighting he asked, 'Is there any real progress that I can report to Sir James, Mr Holmes? I am sure he will be most surprised to discover that you have not, so far, requested an interview with Tordelli's fiancée!'

'I should be glad if you would have her at the hotel no later than six o'clock tomorrow evening. By then, I think your most singular problem will be close to resolution. Cabby!' Holmes rapped the roof of our cab with the top of his cane.

Our driver responded immediately, so drowning out Crawford's increasingly distant protestations.

'Really Holmes! You cannot continually ride roughshod over everyone. Crawford was barely clear of the cab, when you dismissed it and could well have been injured,' I protested.

Holmes was totally oblivious, however, for he was now transfixed by the poster advertising 'Don Giovanni' at the front of the Opera House.

'I am a witless amateur, Watson, not fit to share your cab. I should have noticed the beard before. Now then, a visit to

Savile Row, two wires from the nearest office and the rest of the evening shall be our own. I trust you would not object to dinner at Simpson's,' he proposed, knowing full well that Simpson's was one of my favourite eateries.

'Yes, that would be most agreeable,' I enthusiastically replied. 'I trust however, you will share some of your theories with me before then. I freely admit that I am no more enlightened than I was before we arrived at Covent Garden.'

'You know my method well, Watson,' Holmes began. 'I suggest you now apply it to these few known and relevant facts. A brilliant young baritone disappears from his dressing room after two outstanding performances. He knows no one in this country save the two Covent Garden officials, so both personal and professional reasons for his disappearance can be disregarded. However, his fiancée announces her imminent arrival just hours before he absconds.'

'Obviously he was trying to avoid meeting his fiancée, if you discount the kidnapping theory,' I responded.

'My dear Watson, you surpass yourself! There can be no other explanation. The evidence of the young man at the stage-door totally dismisses any thought of kidnapping. You see, our well-intentioned constabulary continually question the wrong people. Whilst they are wasting time trying to locate an Italian interpreter in order to communicate with Tordelli's fiancée, I already know she can shed no more light on the matter than that news vendor by the corner. Furthermore, whilst they chose to interview the rather pompous stage-door commissionaire, I prefer to chat to his somewhat younger and far more informative assistant. This assistant just happened to hail a cab for a bearded gentleman at the stage-door around the time of Tordelli's supposed disappearance.'

'Supposed?!' I exclaimed, now totally bemused. 'Now Holmes, whatever . . . '

'I used the word 'supposed', Watson, for I am now almost certain of his present whereabouts, and am equally sure he will remain there until tomorrow evening.'

At this moment our hansom pulled up

at the northern end of Savile Row and Holmes immediately alighted.

'Be a good fellow,' he said, handing me two sheets of paper, 'send off these wires and make your way to Baker Street where I will meet you in time for dinner.'

Holmes was as good as his word and we both enjoyed an excellent meal. The only blemish on the evening, as far as I was concerned, was Holmes's absolute refusal to discuss the case and especially his work of that afternoon.

The fact that I knew the contents of his wires did nothing to enlighten me, indeed, the inmost singular lines of enquiry served only to intensify my sense of frustration. The first was to an operatic festival in Bavaria, which merely required an affirmation of the presence of the two gentlemen from Covent Garden. The second requested a list of any unsolved murders and disappearances that had occurred recently in or around Milan.

Despite all my pleas, Holmes refused to be drawn onto the subject but eventually I found myself being calmed by his most eloquent and informative analysis of recent Bruch and Brahms violin concertos. Despite my ignorance of the finer points of violin works, I found my future appreciation of these particular pieces was greatly enhanced as a result of Holmes's analysis.

At the evening's close, my last attempt at extracting information from Holmes met the same fate as my earlier ones.

'I think, my dear Watson, an early night will be of greater benefit to us, for I am sure by morning the game will, most certainly, be afoot.' The faint trace of a smile played briefly on his thin lips, as he perceived my failed attempt at concealing my annoyance and with a shrug, I bade him a curt goodnight and returned to my room.

Despite Holmes's sound advice, I found myself unable to sleep and I soon realized that Holmes was in a similar predicament, for a glimmer of light continued to creep under my door and the faint aroma of tobacco played at my nostrils.

When I eventually surfaced in the morning, Holmes still sat as I had left him the night before and his haggard face bore every sign of a night totally bereft of sleep.

'Holmes!' I exclaimed, 'I must protest at this flagrant and, as far as I can tell, unnecessary abuse you have subjected yourself to. All your plans are well in hand, so why the all night vigil?'

His tired eyes looked up at me, his head moving slightly and unnervingly slowly. 'You are quite right Watson, as far as I was concerned all the pieces were coming together splendidly and yet, it occurred to me as I was about to retire, that all my theories will either stand or fall on the results of the replies to my wires. If they should now prove contrary to my expectations I may well have put lives at risk. I have instructed Mrs Hudson to bring up the replies as soon as they arrive. I shall have only coffee for breakfast.'

I realized that any protest about his non-partaking of food would fall on deaf ears and reluctantly I went on my errand.

After we had breakfasted, Holmes on

coffee, I on toast, marmalade and tea, we spent some of the most torturous hours that I have yet experienced.

The lines of frustration and impatience contorted, still further, his already tired and exhausted features and his consumption of cigarettes was almost incessant as he continually paced up and down the room.

I sat in anguish watching the inner turmoil of Holmes reveal itself as it ate away at him. Again and again, as he passed the bureau, I saw him fingering the handle of the drawer, the one I knew to contain his syringe and cocaine bottle. Yet on each occasion his stronger, professional intent prevented him from feeding his terrible habit and dulling the faculties he knew would soon be needed at their sharpest.

The vigil finally ended at about half-past-one when Mrs Hudson arrived, somewhat breathlessly, in our rooms. With a bound Holmes was across the room to meet her, snatching the telegram from her hand as he hustled her out. Over the years Mrs Hudson's tolerance of such behaviour and abuse had never ceased to amaze me.

'Watson, quickly, see here, how my line of enquiry is at last bearing fruit. Ha!' he exclaimed. 'It is exactly as I thought.'

Yet by the time I had reached his side he had already crumpled the paper in his hand and nonchalantly deposited it in the waste-paper basket.

'Now really Holmes, you go too far!' I exclaimed.

Holmes looked at me furtively from the corner of one eye.

'Very well Watson, you are quite right. We may have yet, I think, a little time before my second reply arrives. Time perhaps for a pipe and a chance for me to air my thoughts on this affair, such as they are.'

Holmes reached for his Persian slipper containing his tobacco, and we each took our customary chairs as he began.

'As you know, Watson, at the start I was somewhat reluctant to take up this challenge. Sir James's arrogant manner and the apparent tedium of a missing person case had almost caused me to choose the boredom of total inactivity to the drudgery of such an undertaking. One most singular point and none other, brought about my change of mind.'

'It was when Sir James mentioned Tordelli's fiancée,' I interrupted excitedly, 'the more so when he mentioned that her imminent arrival had been announced before Tordelli's disappearance. However, I fail to see . . . '

Holmes gave a long draw on his pipe, and then pointed his left finger as he spoke, as if conducting one of his beloved violin concertos! 'Two things occurred to me at once. The fiancée was convinced her arrival would be most welcome; why else should she announce it by telegram. Obviously there were no difficulties between them when she left Italy and obviously none occurred in this country for they had still to meet.

'No, without doubt the problem lies within Tordelli. His reluctance to greet his fiancée is so great that he has put at risk a potentially brilliant career. The reason for this aversion to his fiancée is the one aspect of the case that raises it above the distinctly ordinary. In such a situation, bathed in the warm glow of triumph, yet amongst strangers and away from home, there was no feasible explanation for Tordelli's avoidance of her. So, therefore, having discounted all impossible and improbable theories, I was left, finally, with the truth. The man we are searching for is not Roberto Tordelli!'

I sat bolt upright at this statement and became conscious of my mouth gaping open. 'Then who,' I began, admittedly with a trace of sarcasm in my voice, 'has been singing Don Giovanni these past two nights, at Covent Garden. I am sure Sir James is aware of the identity of his stars.'

'Ah, but that is the point Watson, neither Sir James nor Crawford had ever laid eyes on Tordelli and merely assumed the young baritone with the brilliant voice was who he claimed to be. The reply to my first telegram confirms that only one of Sir James's agents arrived at the festival in Bavaria, the other has, I fancy, been bribed rather handsomely. I must admit I became curious as to the true identity of

Tordelli when I examined the trousers from his theatrical costume. You may not have noticed, but around the waistband were deep and pronounced creases of the type usually associated with an over-tight fit. As a rule, these are produced over a long period of time, as with your own.'

I peered down with some embarrassment at a waistline, which, although quite trim, had increased by some half an inch, since the suit had been tailored for me. Unsuccessfully hiding his amusement at my obvious discomfort, Holmes continued . . .

'These lines were produced in only two nights, therefore, Tordelli's trousers must have been most uncomfortable, to say the least. Curious when you consider they were tailored from the exact measurements wired from Italy. To confirm my theory, I examined the trousers in Tordelli's hotel wardrobe. They all had perfectly flat waistbands. My visit to Savile Row this afternoon, confirmed that no mistakes had been made with the measurements.'

'As usual, your chain of logic is

flawless, Holmes, but at the beginning you mentioned two singular items which were drawn to your attention. I recall your examination of the trousers and seem to remember your mentioning further evidence in the dressing room.'

'I must confess, I nearly missed it myself, yet as we were leaving . . .'

'Of course!' I interrupted, 'the ash tray. I presumed there must have been signs of its recent use. Smoking, of course, is unheard of in an opera singer.'

'Excellent Watson, your powers of observation will soon be surpassing my own.'

For a brief moment these words filled me with overwhelming pride, until I realized there were traces of sarcasm in that familiar voice.

'Someone had taken some care in removing any traces of ash, but they were not entirely successful. I found the faint remnants of a cigarette tobacco unique to Southern Italy. This discovery soon led me down two separate lines of thought, which eventually converged in a most illuminating and yet sinister manner.

‘My interview with the lad at the stage-door and the maid at the hotel, together with the question of the beard all point to one final and clear conclusion, do they not?’

‘Well,’ I began, ‘I am not sure, Holmes. There are still one or two points that need clarification.’

‘Once again, Watson, you have demonstrated, with great effect, your talent for stating the obvious, but any further enlightenment will have to await our meeting with Sir James and Bradstreet at Tordelli’s hotel. For unless I am very much mistaken Mrs Hudson is hastening up the stairs with my second reply.’

Such was his eagerness, that Holmes had already opened the door before Mrs Hudson had reached our landing.

‘A cab, if you please, Mrs Hudson and some cold supper for seven o’clock, if that is agreeable to you, Watson?’

I merely shook my head in disbelief, ‘I am still no closer to solving the problem in my own mind, yet you are already planning the time of your first meal after its conclusion.’

I turned to see that Holmes was oblivious to my words. He read through his telegram, and then screwed it into the pocket of his jacket, which he was already pulling on.

'It seems my worst fears are confirmed, Watson, please make haste and I think your revolver may be of use this evening.'

At these words my heart skipped a beat and the thrill of adventure was upon me once again.

In a moment, we were down the stairs, into a cab and careering down Baker Street towards the great thoroughfare of London.

We reached the hotel lobby a few minutes before six, our appointed time, yet found Bradstreet, Crawford and Sir James already present.

'Gentlemen!' Holmes called loudly, as he raced ahead and up the central stairs. 'To the second floor!'

'Second floor?' Bradstreet muttered and we all exchanged questioning glances. Then, not wanting to appear ignorant of my friend's motives, I confirmed the order. 'To the second floor then!' And led the way for the rest of them.

We found Holmes and the young assistant manager at the door of suite number twenty-four.

'Bradstreet, you and Watson follow closely behind me with your firearms at the ready.' Then turning to the assistant manager, 'I trust you have the pass key? Surprise is crucial if we are to avoid bloodshed.'

With a shaking hand the young man nervously produced the key from an inside pocket and handed this to Holmes before slowly backing away. Holmes motioned to Bradstreet and myself to close ranks behind him as he silently inserted the key and for Sir James, Crawford and the assistant manager to hold back until the room was rendered secure.

No sound was audible from within, as we waited for Holmes to open the door and for one awful, but inconceivable moment I feared Holmes had miscalculated and that his prey had flown the coop. For what seemed an interminable length of time, though it was in fact little more than five minutes, Holmes stood there listening, with his left ear pressed firmly to the door. Bradstreet and I stood as statues, weapons at the ready and prepared to answer Holmes's bidding. However, I overheard from our companions, positioned further along the corridor, a few peppery, and impatient mutterings that threatened the success of our mission. I motioned them to silence as I saw Holmes finally turn the key.

Suddenly, upon noticing the open door, one of the room's occupants shouted excitedly to his companion in Italian. Holmes's next movement was as rapid as it was direct. Bradstreet and I barely had time to draw breath, let alone take action, before Holmes had leapt into the room and into a tackle with a large, bearded man on his way to the door.

The surprise as much as the force of Holmes's attack, floored the bearded man with ease, but the man was both large and strong and was soon back on his feet. Then the two men began circling each other, the large bearded Italian assuming the pose of a bare-knuckle boxer, while

Holmes readied himself in the time honoured position of the Baritsu wrestler. As these two prepared for combat, Bradstreet and I were deciding on how best to intervene, when events took a further, unexpected turn. A most singular looking couple now appeared at the door to the suite.

The man's appearance was decidedly continental, bedecked as he was in an uncomfortably tight-looking grey suit and a dapper light grey bowler perched on top of his tiny head. A huge black moustache completed the bizarre appearance of the man, I was soon to discover, was his companion's interpreter. His companion was most striking indeed. She was tall and slim, in fact, she towered over the interpreter and her facial beauty was almost classical in its intensity. Her most striking feature, however, was her wondrous jet-black hair, which framed this beauty; her full red lips completed her marvellous countenance. She was flushed with fear and excitement at the events now unfolding before her and gabbled incessantly in her native Italian.

Then to my great surprise and horror, Holmes turned his gaze from his opponent for an instant, to ascertain the source of this new drama. With an agility, astonishing in so large a man, the bearded Italian was upon Holmes at once, felling and momentarily winding him with a single kick to the stomach. I cursed myself for failing to react as quickly as I should have, so shocked was I at seeing Holmes so incommoded. The Italian, however, lost no time in wrapping his huge arm around the fragile neck of the young girl and he backed away from us screaming unintelligibly in the most threatening of tones. By now Holmes had struggled to his feet, still nursing his abdomen, but was rooted to the spot as any action on his part would surely have jeopardised the girl's life. The interpreter explained that if we let him flee with the girl as hostage he would release her once he was safely away. To emphasise the point, the large Italian applied a firmer grip to the girl's neck to the point where she was struggling for breath.

A quick glance at Holmes confirmed

that he was now fully recovered and I gestured towards the pocket, which held my revolver. Holmes shot me a half smile before letting out a most violent scream. Then, clutching his stomach, as if still in much pain, he staggered towards the Italian and his struggling captive. The Italian turned to look at Holmes affording me the opportunity to steal up behind the huge man and then bring my revolver crashing down upon the back of his skull. Whilst emitting the anguished roar of a wounded tiger, the large Italian clutched at his bleeding head, and his eyes started to roll back, as he crashed onto the parquet floor, unconscious.

The much relieved girl then spun away from him and into my arms. I helped her to a chair and poured her some water from a carafe on the side table.

'A smart bit of work there, Doctor,' Bradstreet acknowledged, whilst slapping me heartily on the back. 'Your action certainly averted a potentially dangerous situation.'

I turned to find Holmes standing beside me, smiling proudly. 'Bravo Watson!' he exclaimed, shaking my hand energetically. 'Your timing, as always, was impeccable.'

I felt overcome whilst savouring every moment of so rare an event . . . a compliment from Mr Sherlock Holmes! I acknowledged this with the briefest of bows, and he turned his attention, once more, to the matter in hand.

Seeing that all was now secure in the ante-room, Holmes immediately dived into the inner suite, only to find his second, would-be opponent sitting passively in a chair. This individual was also bearded, but there any similarity between him and his companion ended. Although he was seated with his back to us, facing the window, he was evidently much younger and slimmer than the boarish giant I had just felled. Upon hearing us unceremoniously enter his room, the man turned round briefly, displaying a surprising lack of interest until the young beauty, Signora Calvinni joined us in the room. Then he became most agitated, jumping up from his chair and, evidently, calling for his incapacitated associate. Then, upon realizing that the giant would not be coming to his rescue and that his situation was a hopeless one, the young man dropped back down into his chair with an air of resignation.

Despite my efforts at restraining her, Signora Calvinni insisted on approaching the young man.

She spoke quickly and with passion. I think the interpreter used some licence in his translation for the number of words she seemed to use far exceeded those translated.

'But where is he? Where is my beloved Roberto?'

'Yes Holmes,' said Sir James, who had also entered the room, 'what is all this tomfoolery, where is Tordelli?'

'Still in Italy, I rather fancy, but we are here this evening to find your missing Don Giovanni!' Holmes exclaimed.

By this time the bearded gentleman, whom Holmes had assailed, had regained his composure and not a little confidence. He was complaining, through his interpreter, to Bradstreet, of his treatment and the intrusion.

Bradstreet, in common with most of his

colleagues, was not averse to a situation whereby my friend might be brought down a peg or two and decided to intervene.

'Now see here, Mr Holmes, this here Italian gentleman claims he and his companion are two very wealthy and respected businessmen. He claims that he only assaulted the young woman out of fear and desperation. He objects most strongly to this treatment and demands the police be sent for. He was most perplexed when I identified myself as one and is somewhat confused.'

'His confusion I can well understand, I am hard pushed myself at times, in identifying you with detection,' Holmes sharply rebutted. As he was speaking, Holmes slowly approached the young Italian, who, by now, was backing away from Signora Calvinni. Holmes was on him in an instant, despite Bradstreet's ardent protestations, however Holmes's back prevented us from seeing the nature of the ensuing struggle. When he next turned to us he was holding a wig or fake beard in his hand, which he held high in triumph.

The clean-shaven young man, whom Holmes had revealed, was clearly distraught.

'Tordelli!' Sir James exclaimed. 'Really Mr Holmes, it would seem that your abilities even outweigh your considerable reputation. I congratulate you, and offer a thousand apologies for my disparaging attitude of before.'

Holmes waved this casually aside, yet stood there for a minute, barely suppressing a smile, enjoying to the full the drama of the moment and Sir James's marked and sudden change in attitude. Bradstreet was visibly crestfallen, but soon decided to regain some authority by withdrawing his notebook and demanding that Holmes relate, in full, his line of enquiry.

This he was only too happy to do, as his questioning of the assistant porter at Covent Garden, which led him to this conclusion, again highlighted the inefficiency of the London police force.

I heard Bradstreet exclaim, 'Two men with beards! Both asking for cabs to take them to the hotel. Well of course, that's straightforward enough.'

Then in the midst of the confusion and noise, we all remembered the unfortunate fiancée of Tordelli. She stood shocked and silent in the centre of the room, tears running down her lightly rouged cheeks. Her interpreter stepped forward.

'Signora Calvinni would like to know the whereabouts of her beloved Roberto,' he said quietly.

'Good heavens!' Sir James exclaimed. 'Is she mad? Why, he stands before her.'

Not for the first time in our association, Holmes's kindness and consideration towards a grief-stricken lady surprised me. For one so averse to associating with women, a situation such as this showed a side to his nature that was rarely seen, even by me.

With a gentle smile, he took her by the hand and led her to an easy chair. Once he was satisfied that she was comfortably seated, he said:

'I very much regret, Signora, that your fiancé has fallen prey to an odious band of organised criminals, commonly known in your country as the Cosa Nostra. The young gentleman here, who has taken his identity, is not entirely to blame however, for his was a simple ambition to be an opera star and he took whatever opportunity the influence of his family might present to him. He felt that crimes of bribery and deception were relatively minor.

'I must point out, however, that even so evil an organisation as the Cosa Nostra would not carry out murder merely to advance the operatic career of one of their family. My reports indicate that Tordelli had been a witness to a murder that they had committed and they are not people who deal lightly with such matters.'

Sir James followed Holmes out, shaking his head at the loss, once again, of his opera star. It was explained to him that Tordelli or rather the impostor Guiseppe Analdo, whilst not being the murderer, would have to stand trial in Milan as an accessory to the fact.

Bradstreet also shook his head, in disbelief.

'It is incredible, Tordelli wasn't missing

at all, and his own hotel was the perfect hiding place.'

'I must, again, thank and congratulate you, Mr Holmes.'

'Not at all, not at all, I merely questioned the two witnesses you, unfortunately, decided to ignore and I was ably assisted by a pair of trousers, some cigarette ash and a beard.'

'Ah yes the beard!' I exclaimed. 'However did you know which one was false?'

'Until we reached the room, I must confess, I could not be sure that either would be. I merely regarded it as possible that the other bearded gentleman leaving Covent Garden was Analdo in his Giovanni guise. When I observed the two beards in close proximity, the truth of my supposition was clear. I have noticed, in my numerous studies of the human race, that very rarely does the facial hair grow to the exact pigment as that on the head. This you can see for yourselves on this individual.' He pointed to the large Italian bodyguard, and there was indeed a subtle difference in shade. 'Analdo's, on the other hand,' Holmes continued, 'was matched too perfectly by Covent Garden's costume department and gave him away immediately.

'Ah, I see your constables are ready to remove our foreign guest. Take especially good care of this fellow,' he said pointing to the bodyguard. 'I fancy he is a dangerous individual and may even yet prove to be Tordelli's murderer.'

Holmes glanced at his watch and announced, 'Watson, I think we now deserve that supper that Mrs Hudson will have so kindly prepared for us, and I trust you will indulge me afterwards and accompany me to what promises to be a rather splendid violin recital at eight o' clock.'

'I should be delighted Holmes, provided there is no singing!'

The Hooded Man

During the early months of my marriage to my dear Mary, I saw precious little of my old friend Sherlock Holmes. My medical practice had been unusually busy due to an outbreak of influenza brought on by an unseasonably mild and wet January. Therefore, though I am ashamed to admit it, I had barely given him a thought. However, when Mary decided to visit her family for a fortnight and a frosty cold snap stemmed my influx of patients, my thoughts turned once more to 221b Baker Street.

So it was, that on a particularly frosty February morning I found myself staring up, once more, at that familiar building. I hesitated for a moment, unsure of the reception I might receive from my unpredictable friend, however Mrs Hudson's cheery greeting helped alleviate these fears and I bounded up the stairs to our old rooms.

I found Holmes seated on the window ledge with his back to the door. I had not expected a warm greeting from him, but Holmes reacted to my presence as if I had not been away. He merely waved me towards him, barely giving me a glance.

'Come and watch the poor career of a redundant crime specialist disappear down a London thoroughfare,' he said quietly. I noted at least three days' hair growth on his gaunt face and knew at once that he was bemoaning the lack of a stimulating case.

I joined him at the window and followed his forlorn gaze down Baker Street. While Holmes sat there shaking his head, I tried to observe the cause of his mood. Yet all I could see was the usual throng of hundreds of Londoners making their way to work. There was nothing noteworthy about any of them. I told Holmes as much.

'Exactly Watson!' Holmes exclaimed. 'Ordinary people going about their ordinary lives, not one of them possessing that divine spark of genius or inspiration to challenge an extraordinary detective.'

Holmes's immodesty had often annoyed me in the past, but in this context it seemed to be in very poor taste.

'Well, I hope that not one of them would agree with you.'

'Perhaps you are right, Watson; one unemployed detective is a small price to pay for a crime-free metropolis. Ah! Mrs Hudson has your breakfast.' He opened the door before Mrs Hudson had a chance to knock and ushered her in bearing a large tray.

'Doctor Watson, I have prepared something special for your visit and I do hope you can persuade Mr Holmes to join you. He barely eats enough to fill a sparrow.' Mrs Hudson left the tray on the table and hurried out before Holmes could remonstrate with her.

'Spare me your disapproval Watson,' Holmes anticipated, 'I had every intention of indulging in a slice or two of toast and a cup of coffee, prior to your impromptu visit.'

'Well looking at you, I would say it was long overdue,' I said while uncovering the dishes. I soon applied myself to some delicious bacon and eggs, while Holmes sat there, suppressing an amused smile.

'I am glad to observe that married life has done nothing to suppress your appetite. So, Watson, will your sabbatical allow you time to sample some fresh Kentish sea air for a few days?'

'I am sure it would,' I replied between mouthfuls, 'but in heaven's name why?'

'Despite my appearance and my disparaging remarks about our humdrum fellow Londoners, the wheels are turning once again.' Holmes reached into his dressing gown pocket and produced three pages of a crumpled letter, which he tossed onto the table by my plate. 'Ha! Now chew on that, friend Watson!'

Dear Mr Holmes,

Before I begin, please accept my apologies for troubling you on something which I am sure you will think is trivial. I would not have done so, even now, but Inspector Hopkins of the Kent Police insisted this was not a police matter, as no crime had been committed, and he suggested I wrote to you.

'Inspector Hopkins again!' I exclaimed, putting aside the letter for a moment. 'His commission has introduced us to five or six of your most successful cases, even that affair of the Abbey Grange, which began so disappointingly, was something special.'

'Ah yes the three glasses and the remarkable Captain Crocker!' Holmes agreed and then waved towards the letter. 'Please continue.'

I will try to be as brief as possible. My situation is this:

My ailing mother and I run a small boarding house, 'Cliff Court Lodge', perched on the steepest of the harbour cliffs, looking down on Broadsea Bay. Apart from Nellie, our live-in housemaid and two elderly permanent lodgers, we are the only occupants of this large, draughty house.

As you can imagine, our livelihood depends on our having a successful summer season, and therefore I can offer you nothing more than your rail fare to Broadsea Bay and the best hospitality Cliff Court Lodge can offer.

Now, to blind old Captain Dyson. Sixteen years ago, a period in my life still vivid, because it was at this time that my dear father passed away, there was a tragic fire on board the 'Sea Lizard'. This was the largest and finest vessel in our trawler fleet, and was owned by Captain Dyson. An accident occurred in the engine-room whilst the vessel was still in harbour and the fire consumed the entire ship's company save the captain.

Despite the gravity of the captain's injuries, he lost the use of his left arm and had hideous facial burns which left him blinded and horribly deformed, the people of our village despised him for having survived whilst his crew perished. He was shunned, made an outcast and from then until now, Captain Dyson has shut himself away in his small shack on the cliff, adjacent to our property. Whenever he leaves his place, his entire head is shrouded in a large black hood.

Apart from the Widow McCumber, who cleans for him once a week out of pity, no-one visits the shack. He only comes out of it once a day when he shuffles slowly down the narrow path to the harbour, using a long staff to guide his way. People avoid the path when they hear the echo of his stick upon the cobble and he meets no-one on his route.

Out of respect for who he once was, Linus Rawlings, the Landlord of 'The Admiral's Mast' tavern, provides him with ham, cheese and a small cask of ale in exchange for a few coins. The patrons all turn from him when he enters and the transaction takes place in an eerie silence. Dyson slowly returns to his shack, clasping his precious supplies and tapping his staff, there to remain until the following day.

My room faces towards the harbour, so it is not uncommon for me to see Captain Dyson on his return trip, always at five o'clock in the afternoon, *when I take to my room to read.*

You can imagine my surprise, Mr Holmes, when last Tuesday, as I was leaving my room at six o'clock to serve supper, I glanced out of my window and saw Captain Dyson coming up the path towards our house, I was suddenly struck by how menacing the hood made him appear, I must confess this feeling was compounded by the thought of what lay beneath. As I stood watching him, Dyson altered his schedule further by continuing straight up the path, rather than branching to the right towards his shack as he normally would do. Just in front of our house the path branches again, left to our entrance and right towards the original path and Dyson's shack.

I was relieved and thankful to see him bear to the right and I left my window to organise supper. Before leaving my room, however, I was stopped in my tracks by a sound; or rather a lack of one, Dyson had stopped tapping the path with his staff.

Hesitantly I returned to my window and Captain Dyson had halted directly beneath me. Now, I understand that you might think these are the ramblings of a mad woman and burn this letter when you continue to read, but Dyson seemed to be standing there gazing up at me! Impossible for a blind man, and you would think just my imagination, yet, Mr Holmes, despite his large black shroud the Captain was standing there staring up at me. Finally, when I moved from the window I heard the tapping resume and he finally returned to his shack.

Mr Holmes, he has repeated this pattern every day since, each time lingering a while longer beneath my window and I have not had a night's sleep since. Captain Dyson's eyes were seared from their sockets in the fire so why does he seem to be watching me? What does it mean?

If your schedule allows, I would be so grateful if you would come to Broadsea and put my mind at rest. You will be made very welcome at our

Lodge and I hope to see you at your earliest convenience.
Lucy Hardcastle,
Cliff Court Lodge.

Holmes was now leaning eagerly across the table like a pointer dog held on its leash, awaiting my reaction to this most singular letter.

'Has there ever been a more heartfelt cry for your help?' I asked.

'It is most gratifying, I admit, but what is your theory friend Watson? I am sure this Captain Dyson has not found himself a new pair of eyes.' Holmes quipped, lighting yet another cigarette.

'I must confess I am at a complete loss,' was my bland reply.

'You are intrigued though, admit it.'

'Of course!' I confirmed.

'Intrigued enough to accompany me to the Kent coast?'

'I would not dream of letting you go alone.'

'Capital Watson! Our train leaves Victoria in fifty-five minutes!'

I nearly choked on my tea. 'Our train!

Really Holmes, this time you have presumed too much!'

'Calm yourself, Watson, you know I cannot resist a touch of melodrama. However the truth is I visited your home last week and, though disappointed to find you engaged at your surgery, I enjoyed a delightful tea with Mrs Watson. She informed me of her planned fortnight away with her family. So, you can see that your visit this morning was not entirely unexpected.'

'Even so . . . ' Yet I was so amused by his presumptuousness that I could not persist with my objections.

'Do you still keep your overnight bag packed and in readiness?' Holmes asked.

'Of course.'

'Excellent! We shall collect them on our way to Victoria.' Holmes disappeared into his room and in an instant emerged clothed in his heavy ulster and deer-stalker.

'Cab, Mrs Hudson!' He called as he bundled me out of the room. Still bemused as to how a surprise visit to my old lodgings had turned around so, I now found myself on my way to a new adventure in Kent.

As we alighted from our train, I was immediately struck by the effect of a North Sea breeze on an already intensely cold February day. Clearly Holmes was similarly affected for we turned our coat collars up to our cheeks simultaneously.

We followed the directions furnished by the station master and ten minutes later found ourselves outside Cliff Court Lodge.

As we stood waiting for a response to our knock on the door, I quickly surveyed our surroundings. The picturesque harbour nestling in a secluded bay, the small row of shops which comprised the high street and a small dilapidated building perched on an adjacent cliff. Even from this distance I could see the wood was rotten and its roof was covered with moss.

'Holmes, look! Dyson's shack.' I pointed. Holmes, however, was more intent on escaping the freezing wind to which he was more susceptible than I, and ignoring my observation, banged his way into the Lodge in search of a relieving fire.

To compensate for Holmes's brusqueness, I tipped my hat to the round-faced young woman, whom I rightly assumed was the maid Nellie, who had just opened the door to us. 'Mrs Hardcastle and Miss Lucy are waiting for you in the drawing-room at the end of the passage; I shall be along presently with some tea, gentlemen.' Holmes was already half way down the passage, so I thanked the girl and followed him at a more sedate pace.

The drawing-room proved to be a small, yet comfortably furnished room with a large roaring fire by which Holmes had settled himself in a comfortable chair and was holding his hands by the warming coals. Unfortunately Mrs Hardcastle had taken to her bed suffering with a mild headache, her daughter's welcome, however, more than compensated for her mother's absence. Lucy Hardcastle was a small slim young woman with light brown curly hair, loosely tied with a ribbon. She leapt from her chair the moment we entered the room.

'Oh, Mr Holmes, I cannot believe someone so celebrated would come to my aid so promptly. Thank you so much, and you too, Dr Watson!'

Clearly embarrassed, Holmes waved her aside as she attempted to grasp his hands. He was saved further awkwardness by Nellie's timely arrival with a tea-trolley.

The tea was sweet, strong and piping hot, and after two cups, Holmes finally felt able to remove his outer garments.

'Miss Hardcastle, your letter was both informative and coherent. Is there anything you have omitted which you feel might aid my investigation?' Holmes asked, leaning forward towards her.

She hesitated for a moment. 'No, I do not think so. I should warn you, however, that my mother was most averse to my sending the letter, if there are any questions you wish to ask of her, might I suggest you wait until the morning.'

'A most commendable idea, Miss Hardcastle, now if we can be shown to our rooms, I should like to take a walk while there is still some daylight.'

'Nellie will take you to your rooms on the first floor, close to my own, no doubt you will then visit Captain Dyson's shack?'

'All in good time, but I think an evening at the 'Admiral's Mast' would be far more informative. Do not, I pray, prepare supper on our account.'

As Holmes left the room, Miss Hardcastle glanced quizzically at me.

'In the past Mr Holmes has gained more information from a visit to a public house than he could get from a dozen interrogations,' I explained as I followed Holmes to our rooms. Within a few minutes we were on the path leading down to the harbour.

I was always annoyed by the ease with which Holmes adapted to so many diverse environments, for, within a few moments, the patrons were eating out of his hands.

'A tankard of your finest ale please, landlord,' He began, and then in a louder voice; 'and one for each of your fine clientele who wish to join me.'

The decision to do so was unanimous and soon tongues loosened by alcohol were filling up my notebook with tales of the 'Sea Lizard' and Captain Dyson.

'A Captain should be the last off the vessel, not the first,' said one.

'He was a great sailor, yet a captain without honour is of no use,' said another; and so it continued, well into the evening.

After a while, I noticed Holmes's distraction from his entourage, as he became aware of one isolated character, seated in a corner by the door.

He was small of stature, yet his great coat and muffler obscured his features. He savoured each sip of his rum and his cigarette seemed to last an eternity. Then, when both were consumed, the man silently slipped out into the night. A movement from Holmes's head urged me to follow this character while Holmes remained, out of courtesy to his new friends, for a final drink.

The path outside was ill-lit and this, together with a sea mist drifting languidly in from the harbour, rendered my pursuit of this mysterious stranger a blind and futile exercise.

Then, from ahead and to the right, I

heard the sound of leather and studs scuffing on stone, so I followed the sounds and not the sight of this man as he made his way towards Dyson's shack.

As I drew closer, the shack began materialising through the gloom and mist, although still an indistinct oblong shape. Then, the scuffing sound ceased and I stood still, rooted to the spot, unsure of how and where to proceed.

I soon regretted my decision to remain where I was, when a vice-like grip held the right shoulder of my coat. Instinctively my left hand reached into my coat pocket, wherein the reassurance of my revolver lay.

'Calm yourself, Watson. For tonight at least, gun play will not be required. Our bird has truly flown.'

'Holmes! Will you always get amusement from unnerving me?' Before he answered I suggested we continue our pursuit as we were now so close to Dyson's shack.

'Come, Watson. We shall learn much more in daylight, and besides, I have gorged myself on information that requires much digestion.'

Reluctantly I followed Holmes back to the lodge.

'Holmes,' I ventured as we walked. 'Could you at least explain to me, what we have learned tonight?'

Holmes had evidently begun his digestion process, so oblivious was he to my question. We continued in silence and did not communicate further until breakfast the following morning.

I entered the dining room at a little after eight o'clock and found it to be a bright, cheery room, full of dried flower arrangements and small, rural landscapes. The elderly residents were enjoying a rack of toast and pot of tea and Holmes, the room's only other occupant, was seated at a small corner table, partaking of a cigarette, coffee and, by the look of the table, very little else.

'Good morning Holmes, does not even the sea air produce in you a sufficient appetite so you can enjoy a proper breakfast? You'll fade away before long.'

Holmes could not contain his amusement and he was chuckling to himself as he blew smoke from his nostrils.

'Your comments on my eating habits are clearly based on the sparsity of my table. Although your efforts at observation and deduction are commendable, in as far as they go, a closer examination of the tablecloth should have revealed the consumption of a full and satisfying breakfast.' He pointed to an egg-yolk stain, and toast crumbs, dotted around. 'The empty dishes were removed by Nellie only seconds before you entered the room.'

Stifling my embarrassment, I sat down opposite him. 'Well, as your friend and doctor, I am certainly glad my deduction was so inaccurate.' As I spoke Nellie bustled towards me, and I ordered kippers, toast and a pot of tea.

'So, Watson,' Holmes began, while I awaited my food, 'what relevant information did we glean from our visit to the inn yesterday evening?'

'Well, we certainly confirmed the contents of Miss Hardcastle's letter, where she describes Dyson's current standing in the village. I have never heard such unanimous hostility toward a single member of a small community. To a man they hold him responsible for the deaths of his crew.'

'Indeed, though that issue was never really in doubt. As usual, however, you have been drawn towards the more sensational gossip of the general conversation. I, on the other hand, assimilate only those small gems that often get lost in the general mêlée, yet prove vital at the conclusion. For example, I established that Mrs McCumber is not the paragon of virtue that she would have us believe.

'She does not clean for Captain Dyson out of pity, she tends to him out of affection, for they were once fervent lovers and she spends a lot more time at the shack than it could possibly take to clean it.'

My food had arrived during the course of this statement, and a mouthful of kipper precluded my making any comments.

'However,' Holmes continued, 'the most interesting aspect of Mrs McCumber is her regular monthly visits to

London, ostensibly to visit an aged aunt and always lasting for four days. This month, however, she went for a week and has still not returned.'

'Yes, but why should Mrs McCumber interest you so?' I asked.

Lighting a cigarette, in a lowered voice, he said. 'She also happens to be Nellie's mother . . . ' As he spoke, Nellie herself, redder of face than usual, bustled into the room in a state of agitation, preceding a familiar figure.

Saving her having to announce the arrival, Holmes called out, 'Ah, Inspector Hopkins, will you not join us for some tea?'

'Good morning, gentlemen,' Hopkins gravely responded, extending his hand to each of us. 'But I am afraid on this occasion I have no time for tea. I cannot believe my good fortune, in that you responded positively to Miss Hardcastle's entreaties.'

'Her letter was most persuasive.' Holmes replied. 'However, I understood that her little conundrum held no interest for the Kentish police.'

'That was certainly true before this morning's tragic occurrence. You see, gentlemen, Captain Dyson has been found dead on the beach!'

'Good heavens! Was it an accident? Did he fall?' I asked excitedly.

Hopkins slowly shook his head. 'I am afraid it is far too early to say, Doctor. We shall know more after we have made our initial examination.'

'Am I to understand that no one has yet trampled over the scene of the crime?' Holmes asked.

'Apart from the early morning limpet hunter, who discovered Dyson, no one has attended the body, nor has the site on the cliff top been disturbed. It would appear that the body was pushed from there. The scene is as untouched and pristine as a man of your unique talents could wish it.'

Gleefully, Holmes clapped his hands and rose hurriedly from his chair. 'Capital Hopkins! We shall, of course accompany you at once.' Then he glanced down at my half eaten kipper, and the expectant fork in my left hand, and with surprising consideration, offered to collect our coats, while allowing me to complete my meal. Gratefully, I attacked my fish once more. Holmes's magnanimity was short lived however and in a few moments he called out impatiently.

'Do hurry along, Watson!'

A few minutes later Holmes, Inspector Hopkins and I were striding purposefully towards the cliff top to the right of Dyson's shack. Immediately, I was struck by how oblivious the scent of the hunt had rendered Holmes to the severity of the weather. This was, indeed, far harsher than it had been on the previous day.

As we came within thirty yards of the edge of the cliff, Holmes suddenly stopped in his tracks, and bade us do the same.

'Inspector!' Holmes called; he had to raise his voice to be heard above the stiffening breezes, 'What is the exact location of Dyson's body in relation to the top of the cliff?'

In front of us was spread a wide expanse of unkempt grass. To our right it ran directly down to the harbour behind the line of small shops and cottages that were terraced along the harbour road. To our left the grass extended to Dyson's shack and beyond, while straight ahead of us it grew right up to the edge of the cliff, and the oblivion below.

Hopkins pointed to a small rise, marked out by a clump of bramble bushes. Holmes followed the direction of Hopkins's straightened arm.

'The body was discovered lying spread-eagled on its back, directly below that point over there,' Hopkins called back.

'And you are certain that none of your men have, so far, set foot on this grass?' Holmes asked anxiously once more.

'Mister Holmes, I have despatched four Constables to cordon off Dyson's grotesque form from the curious public gaze. We are the first to arrive here.'

'Excellent!' Holmes beamed. 'Once again, Inspector, your conduct has proved exemplary. Now I beseech you gentlemen to take no steps further forward until I have fully examined this untamed stretch of turf.'

Hopkins and I duly pulled up our coat

collars in anticipation of a long, cold vigil. We were fortunate in that Hopkins's foresight had granted us a warm golden glow of cognac from his hip flask. Holmes, however, was fuelled by something far more effective. His love of the hunt.

Initially he advanced slowly, and seemed uninterested in the ground before him. Then he came upon, what we assumed to be a footprint, and in an instant he had laid himself flat on his stomach, his glass automatically appearing in his right hand. He lay there for three or four minutes, slowly passing the glass back and forth over the area immediately ahead of him.

Then, apparently satisfied, with a sudden movement he snapped himself back up to his feet, and began a long range survey by rotating himself slowly, hands on hips, until his next discovery found him once more flat on his front. I could just detect a strange grunting sound of disappointment emanate from him as he jumped up once more. He just stood there pensively pressing his lips with his right forefinger. We next heard a small cry of triumph, and he was on the move again. This time, however, he was following the trail from a vertical position, so positive was he of his interpretation of the traces.

The trail led him to the very edge of the cliff and it was only when he reached the edge that he lay down once more on his front, glasses in hand. For a moment or two he peered over the edge down to the sand below.

I was used to my friend's disregard for his own well-being, but Hopkins clearly thought Holmes was over-reaching himself and called out to him, 'Have a care, Mr Holmes!' Holmes pulled himself back and stood up.

'Do not unduly worry yourself, Inspector, the risk was well worth taking,' he called as he retraced his steps towards us. Then something caught his attention, which he clearly had not expected to find. The look of triumph was now one of great puzzlement as he turned away from us again, this time following a path behind the line of shops and houses that led down to the harbour.

He disappeared from our view for a few minutes.

'It is not often your friend seems so perplexed,' Hopkins remarked. I saw the look on Holmes's face as he came back into view.

'Thankfully, it does not usually last long,' I replied.

'Gentlemen, I must return to London for a couple of days to conclude my investigation.'

This time it was Hopkins and I who looked confused.

'In heaven's name, why London?' I asked.

'Because I have learned all I can down here in Kent,' was Holmes's typically enigmatic reply.

'When do you intend to leave?'

'On the first available train, I believe there is one due to leave in twenty minutes.'

'So soon, do you not even intend to view the body?' Inspector Hopkins asked.

'I shall leave that in your expert hands, although Watson, I think you will find that death occurred five days ago. I commend that fact to you, Inspector, as being most suggestive. Now Watson, in my absence I should rely on you to ensure that Nellie McCumber shall not set foot from the lodge under any circumstance.'

'You may rely on me Holmes, but for what reason? Is her life in danger?'

'The very greatest danger,' Holmes nodded gravely. 'You did not realize her bedroom is directly above that of Miss Hardcastle?'

'I confess I did not, yet how does that endanger her?' I asked.

Clearly Holmes would not be further drawn. 'You have two days to consider the facts and use my methods, then it will become clearer.'

Holmes at once turned on his heels and set off for the station. 'Remember, Watson, she must not leave the lodge, even for an instant!' He called back over his shoulder.

As I watched my friend stride away, I turned to Hopkins for inspiration. He merely shrugged, and turned towards the beach. I returned to the lodge to begin my vigil.

The forty-eight hours that followed passed very slowly for me. The inclement weather left me with no regrets at not being able to step outside, and Nellie displayed no great desire to do so either. This, of course, rendered the task of protecting her that much easier. Holmes's other request, that I use his method in unravelling the murderous demise of Captain Dyson and its connection with the threat to Nellie's life, proved somewhat more difficult.

Therefore, I sat myself before a large fire in the drawing-room and began reading the chronicles of Sir Richard Burton and his fascinating exploits in the wilds of East Africa. Compelling as these were, they failed to retain my attention for very long, and Holmes's parting words were constantly intruding on my concentration.

His startling assertion, that Dyson's body had been thrown from the top of the cliff five days previously began to look more remarkable during the course of my first evening alone. I had just dropped Burton's tome to the floor in frustration, when Inspector Hopkins called briefly at the lodge with the news that the police surgeon had confirmed Holmes's estimate of the time of death.

Hopkins stood before the fire slowly shaking his head. 'Your friend is a remarkable man, Doctor, and a remarkable detective. How could he possibly have gauged the time of Dyson's death without even viewing the body?'

'I have spent the day going over the problem in my mind, and I confess the thing is no clearer to me.' I replied. 'Besides, why should the exact location of Nellie McCumber's bedroom place her life in jeopardy?'

Voraciously rubbing his hands together in the warm glow of the fire, Hopkins slowly replied. 'My own investigations have revealed little themselves, though I believe I can now identify the man you followed from the Admiral's Mast the other evening. Based on your description of him I am certain it was James 'The Weasel' Willis, an old friend of the inn's landlord, Linus Rawlins. Though both men are disreputable, I have, to date, uncovered little of specific note. I shall, of course, inform you of further developments as they occur, but a robbery in Ramsgate will occupy my attention for the next few hours. Goodnight to you, Doctor Watson.'

I showed the industrious Inspector to the door, which I then promptly secured. I ensured that Nellie McCumber was safely asleep before retiring for the night myself.

The night passed slowly for me. A stiff breeze from the North Sea rattled the loose sash on my window, and when I did sleep, images of hooded men, constantly climbing and re-climbing the cliff path, intruded on my slumber. I was much relieved, in the morning, when my small, but satisfying breakfast was brought to my table by Nellie, apparently safe and well.

A moment later Miss Hardcastle, in a state of great agitation, rushed into the room.

'Oh, Doctor Watson, you had better

come quickly! Your Inspector friend is in the process of arresting James Willis for the murder of Captain Dyson.'

'I must speak with him,' I said rising from my dining chair. 'It is a strange action for him to take in the absence of Mr Holmes. I do not intend to be gone for more than a few moments, Miss Hardcastle, but until my return, I beseech you, do not let Nellie out of your sight for an instant.'

'I do wish someone would tell me why I should need protecting.' Nellie murmured.

'I wish I knew myself,' I replied. 'Rest assured, however, once his inquiries are concluded in London, Mr Holmes will have answers to all our questions.'

As I left, outside the lodge I noticed a small group of people gathered by the side of the path. There was a mighty commotion emanating from them, and one of the crowd, in particular, let out the scream of a banshee.

As I drew closer, I realized that the perpetrator of this unholy sound was, of course, James Willis protesting his innocence. His scrawny form was struggling, spread-eagled, on the ground whilst two constables were trying to fit him with handcuffs. I reached Hopkins's side just as they succeeded.

'Good morning Doctor Watson! I thought the sound of our distinguished rogue, here, might drag you from your young charge,' Hopkins greeted me, with not a little irony in his voice.

'Yes, and I must return to her at once. However, I must first know what prompted you to such sudden action. Last evening things were no clearer to you than they were to me.'

In reply, Hopkins pulled a small, crumpled piece of paper from his pocket. He announced: 'A wire from your friend Mr Holmes!'

I read it quickly.

HOPKINS ARREST JAMES WILLIS FOR MURDER OF DYSON STOP DO NOT DELAY STOP HOLMES

'So, he has had success in London it seems. Yet no mention of his imminent return,' I said.

'Well,' Hopkins replied. 'You should know Mr Holmes and his ways better than any of us. In any event, with Willis now safely in custody, you should be able to relax your guard over Miss McCumber.'

'On the contrary,' I replied. 'It is because I know Mr Holmes and his ways so well that I shall not relax my vigil for an instant. Therefore, if there are any further developments you may find me ensconced at the Lodge. Good day to you, Inspector.'

Hopkins doffed his hat in reply, and set to organising the transport of the now silent and crestfallen Willis.

Upon returning to the lodge, I confirmed Nellie's safety before settling myself by the drawing-room fire. The soothing effect of its rising and falling flames, together with the bracing sea air and two sleepless nights, soon lulled my senses. Though I am ashamed to admit it, within a short time I had fallen into a deep sleep.

I was awakened, some three hours later, by a sharp prodding of my left shoulder. As I shook myself from unconsciousness, and rubbed the distortion from my opening eyes, I became aware of a familiar shape bending over me, and a less familiar shape standing tentatively behind the former.

'Watson, it really is too bad of you to greet our guest in such a fashion!' Sherlock Holmes began. 'May I present to you Mrs McCumber, who has very kindly returned with me from London to aid us in concluding this affair.' He introduced her with a flourish of his right hand.

'My humblest apologies, madam,' I said rising from my chair.

'Do not trouble yourself, Watson,' Holmes said. 'The matter is now well in hand. Inspector Hopkins, and his men, are entrenched in the parlour ready to pounce. Even now, a letter I instigated from Miss McCumber is on its way to Dyson's shack, courtesy of the local grocer's boy. As a direct result of this, I expect Dyson's murderer to pay us a visit within the next few minutes.'

'Dyson's murderer?' I exclaimed. 'So it is not James Willis after all! This really is too bad of you, Holmes. Why should a letter from Nellie deliver the murderer into our hands? Why is Hopkins now waiting in the parlour . . . ?' I was interrupted by the sound of crashing metal from outside the window.

'Hush yourself, Watson. Unless I am very much mistaken, that was the sound of the grocer's boy's bicycle crashing to the ground.'

Sure enough, a moment later, a warmly dressed, visibly shaken, twelve-year-old boy scurried into the room.

'I delivered your letter, sir,' the boy breathlessly blurted out. 'As you instructed, I looked behind me as I cycled away, and the gentleman was making his way down the hill.'

'Thank you, Thomas, that is excellent,' Holmes smiled, whilst handing the boy a generous handful of coins. 'Now you had best hurry back to work.'

'Yes sir. Thank you, sir!' the boy cried, upon seeing the coins, and then hurried back to his bike.

'Quickly now,' Holmes instructed. 'Nellie, you take Watson's chair, while the rest of us retire to the adjacent dining-room. The serving hatch will afford us an undetected view of all that transpires.'

We all did his bidding, and Holmes rapped on the parlour wall to alert Hopkins and his men.

The few minutes that followed seemed to take an eternity to pass, hunched as we were by the small aperture of the partially opened serving hatch. Mrs McCumber was obviously anxious and ill at ease, so Holmes placed a comforting hand on her shoulder and whispered: 'Do not fear, I shall allow no harm to come to your daughter.' In this situation, Holmes's voice seemed strangely reassuring, and Mrs McCumber smiled up at him.

Then we heard the sound of footsteps on the gravel outside, and a moment later, when the drawing-room door slowly opened, Holmes tensed, and was ready to pounce on his quarry.

The quarry, however, evidently saw himself as the hunter. As he slowly advanced towards the back of Nellie's chair he clenched, in each hand, the end of a heavy brown scarf. This was pulled taut, in a manner threatening strangulation.

As he drew closer, Linus Rawlins, for it was he who was the intruder, bore an evil grimace on his face that was awful to behold. Then, as he raised his weapon of wool above Nellie's head, Holmes and Hopkins made their move.

Simultaneously they rushed from their respective hiding places, and confronted Rawlins.

'Stay as you are Rawlins!' Holmes ordered. 'Your game is up!'

Cursing profanely under his breath, Rawlins hesitated for a moment, and Mrs McCumber fainted to the floor in shock. Upon realizing that Holmes and Hopkins would be upon him before he could complete his murderous intent, Rawlins turned on his heels, and made towards the drawing-room door, there to be confronted by Hopkins's vigilant constables.

His struggle was as brief as it was futile and he was led back to us by each arm. Then finally, handcuffs secured him, and he was made to sit down before us. By this time Mrs McCumber had recovered sufficiently for her to rejoin us in the drawing-room, and all eyes were now fixed expectantly on Holmes.

His, in turn, were trained aggressively on Rawlins, and he stood defiantly over him, hands on hips, very much like a big game hunter with his foot pressed down on his victim's corpse.

'Inspector,' Rawlins began. 'Who is this gentleman, and why is he bearing over like this?'

'This gentleman,' Hopkins replied, 'happens to be Mr Sherlock Holmes of Baker Street, and the man whose genius you have to thank for saving your neck from the noose!'

'Not so Hopkins,' Holmes rejoined. 'I may have prevented a tragic murder this day, but not the slaying of Captain Dyson some five days earlier. Mr Rawlins shall not escape the hangman for that!'

Rawlins then leapt from his chair, and would surely have attacked Holmes had his wrists not been secured. However the constables took hold of him, once again, and Hopkins had him removed to the local cells, where he would remain until the coroner delivered his report. When he was sure that satisfactory arrangements were in hand, Hopkins returned, and addressed Holmes thus:

'Mr Holmes, we have all witnessed Rawlins's attempted murder here today, yet if I am to secure a murder conviction I shall require more than mere word of mouth, even if that word happens to be yours.'

'Have no fear, Hopkins. I can assure you that, with not a little help from Mrs McCumber, I have constructed a case against Rawlins that will convince the most sceptical of juries.'

As Holmes finished speaking, Miss Hardcastle, and her mother, for once able to vacate her bed, came into the room, and Holmes begged their permission to light up his cherry wood pipe. They acquiesced, and Holmes drew long and hard as he started to speak. I could see from his suppressed smile that Holmes, forever the dramatic showman, was enjoying having an audience.

'Although I am not implying that Miss

Hardcastle deliberately misled me in any way, the irony of this case lies in the fact that the contents of the letter, that first led me to the charming Kentish coast, were based on falsehoods.'

'Mr Holmes, I assure you I was not aware of any, neither at the time of writing the letter nor now,' Miss Hardcastle protested.

'Very likely not,' Holmes continued. 'And yet I am now certain that the man staring up at you, from under the black hood, was not the blinded Captain Dyson, for as the coroner has now ascertained, he was already dead. Nor had he been staring at you, but rather Nellie McCumber, who occupies the room directly above your own.'

'I do not understand,' Miss Hardcastle quietly responded.

'On that point I think we are all in agreement,' said I, feeling frustrated, and not a little hurt at also being kept in the dark.

'A thousand apologies my dear Watson, but rest assured, prior to my trip to London many facets of the case had eluded me also. When I arrived at Victoria I had three intended ports of call. Much time and energy was saved me by my fortuitous encounter with my old friend George just outside the main entrance where he was awaiting his next fare. As Watson will confirm, many times in the past, George's hansom cab and his acute eyes and ears have saved me hours of time wasting leg work, and helped me conclude cases within days rather than weeks. Thankfully he was no less successful on this occasion.'

During the long journey from Victoria station to the maritime records building at Greenwich, I furnished him with a detailed description of Mrs McCumber and a slightly less detailed record of her arrival dates at Victoria over the last few months. By the time I had concluded my perusal of the records and inventories at Greenwich, some three hours later, George had located her to a small spartan hotel at the back of King's Cross. By this time it was too late for me to call upon her, so George returned me to Baker Street where a somewhat surprised, Mrs

Hudson prepared me a little cold supper.

I retired early, as I had instructed George to collect me at eight o'clock the following morning, in order firstly to visit the record's office at Somerset House and to arrive at the hotel in King's Cross before our bird had flown. I was not disappointed. Mrs McCumber was still in her room, though on the point of vacating it when I arrived. After the initial shock of finding me on her doorstep had subsided, and I had explained the purpose of my visit, she relented from her threat to summon the police and invited me into her small, dusty, uncomfortable room.

'In this unenviable setting I told her of everything I had, thus far, ascertained. She, in turn, supplied me with most of the missing details, before agreeing to return with me to Broadsea in time to prevent further tragedy. Inspector, I only lay emphasis on this point in order for you to feel you can deal more leniently with this lady when the whole truth is revealed.'

At that moment Inspector Hopkins turned towards Mrs McCumber, and said solemnly: 'That, madam, very much remains to be seen.' A tearful Mrs McCumber turned away from him while Holmes continued his narrative oblivious of her discomfort.

'I have now told you of every action I took from the moment I left Broadsea two mornings ago, up to the present. Now I will tell you of the reasons behind my actions and all I have learnt as a result of them.'

It was amazing to me, to hear my friend narrate this tale of high drama, with all the dryness and equanimity of a scientist lecturing at the Royal Academy.

He continued: 'It seemed reasonable enough for me to assume that Mrs McCumber's knowledge would be the key to the whole mystery. Her romantic connection to Dyson and the fact that Nellie was her daughter and occupied the room above that of Miss Hardcastle, made it obvious to me that Nellie was the object of the hooded man's attention. The question that nagged at me was why, and I felt sure that Mrs McCumber would be able to furnish me with the answer.'

‘My examination of the area of grass near the cliff’s edge revealed much. I was lucky in that the recent moist weather revealed boot prints and trails that were both clear and distinct, though for that I also have to thank Inspector Hopkins and his diligence.

‘As you may remember, Watson, my initial examination was fruitless, and yet as I drew closer to the edge of the cliff I began picking up definite prints coming from the direction of the shack. One large pair of boots leading the way, and over five feet behind, another, considerably smaller set of footprints. I was also able to observe that the set in front were sunk into the mud to a greater depth than the set behind.’

‘Of course!’ I exclaimed excitedly. ‘The person taking the lead was carrying something of greater weight than the individual who followed. In other words, the leader was carrying the torso, and he who followed was holding the feet!’

‘Excellent Watson! The improvement in your deductive abilities is really most gratifying. However, my discoveries did not end there. My immediate conclusion, that Dyson's murderer was undoubtedly the hooded man who had been so studiously observing the lodge, was borne out by a separate set of footprints I observed on my way back from the cliff. Watson, you may recall my turning away from you and Hopkins at the last, and disappearing down the hill, and behind the shops?'

'I did find it curious at the time, but your departure for London was so sudden that I had little opportunity to raise the point with you,' I replied.

Ignoring my comment, and being swept along by the momentum of his own narrative, Holmes continued.

'In my haste, my own steps almost obliterated another set of prints that, I must confess, even I had not expected to find. This time they were coming from the shack and leading along the route you saw me take towards the harbour. My excitement, at this fresh discovery, was heightened still further when I realized the footprint was the duplicate of that of the torso bearer and, in all probability,

Dyson's murderer. The trail led me directly to an obscure rear entrance to the Admiral's Mast Inn.

'I then retraced my steps towards you with the knowledge that Dyson's murderer and, consequently, the hooded man were undoubtedly one and the same. Furthermore, because the rear door to the inn was securely locked when I attempted entry, this man was, without doubt, Linus Rawlins. His accomplice and the footbearer none other than our friend, James Willis.'

On this occasion it was Hopkins's turn to interrupt my friend's narrative.

'This, of course, explains why you insisted on Willis's immediate arrest, but why should the secure rear door of the inn confirm to you that Rawlins was the culprit?'

'Who but the landlord of such an establishment, would hold the key to so obscure an entrance? You see, the trail led right up to the door, and there were even traces on the step itself,' Holmes replied, with the barest hint of impatience in his voice.

'Ah, now I understand, and, of course, by having Willis arrested for the murder we have secured him for his minor role and lulled Rawlins into a false sense of security at the same time. As usual, Mr Holmes, a masterstroke!'

'Hardly that, Hopkins,' Holmes replied, somewhat dismissively. 'Yet the tracks that led to the back of the inn do explain how Rawlins maintained the façade of Dyson still being alive. Obviously once he had made the return journey from shack to inn, in the guise of the hooded man, he returned to the inn by the back route to reassume his role as the landlord.

'At this point I realized my investigations in Broadsea had run their course. I had established the identity of those who perpetrated Dyson's murder, and all that had occurred subsequently. However the events and motives that led to these were still no clearer to me. Therefore, once having entrusted Nellie's safety into your capable hands, Watson, I decided to return to London and there spent the next forty-eight hours in the manner I previously described to you. Oh, Mrs Hardcastle, might I prevail upon you for a cup of tea. I am finding these endless questions and explanations quite exhausting.'

Mrs Hardcastle responded at once, and a few moments later, when she returned, we were all grateful to see that there was enough tea and sufficient cups for all. During the ensuing, brief lull, Holmes re-lit his cherry wood, and smoked slow and hard. He then drained his cup in an instant, and returned it to the tray before continuing.

'By now the motives behind my calling upon Mrs McCumber at her hotel in King's Cross will be obvious, and self evident. Those behind my journeys to Greenwich, and Somerset House, somewhat less so. Therefore, Inspector, to help clarify the situation, I would ask you to cast your most studious and retentive mind back sixteen years, and attempt to focus on the case of the notorious Folkestone Counterfeit Gang.'

'By heavens, Mr Holmes! I shall have no difficulty in doing that. Despite the great time lapse, that is one file that remains open still. I was only a young, inexperienced Detective Sergeant at the time, working alongside the esteemed Inspector Culver, yet despite our efforts, and six long months of graft, we were never able to bring the ringleaders to book. Furthermore, over half their haul, the best part of sixty thousand pounds in counterfeit twenty-pound notes, was left unaccounted for. The balance of the money and three inconsequential members of the gang were all we had to show for our efforts.' Hopkins appeared somewhat deflated as he recounted his bitter memories.

'You will be pleased to know that, unless I am very much mistaken, the file should soon be finally laid to rest.' Holmes was amused to note the change that came over Hopkins's countenance as he spoke these words.

'It would give me great pleasure to close it finally,' Hopkins responded. 'Yet I see no connection between the two affairs.'

'Do not berate yourself, Hopkins. My visit to London has given me the advantage over you. When I first sat down with the files at the maritime offices in Greenwich, my sole intention was to establish whether there were any noteworthy features connected to the fire on board the 'Sea Lizard'. Something, perhaps, that would supply me with a motive for Dyson's murder. Save the bare-bone facts, already in my possession, the information was scant, to say the least. However, when I idly skipped forward a page or two, I found mention of the raid you made on the hideaway of the counterfeit gang in Folkestone. Normally, such an incident would not find its way into the files at Greenwich as they are restricted to maritime affairs. However, on this occasion it was included because the gang members, who had eluded you, made their escape on board a large steam trawler, of which there were very few at that time.

'As my friend Watson will attest, I am not a man who readily accepts coincidence. I was convinced that the two incidents had to be connected. It was the only logical conclusion, and, to my immense personal gratification, this was confirmed by my visit to Somerset House.'

Sensing an imminent barrage of questions, coming from both the direction of Hopkins and myself, Holmes preempted us, and hastened to his conclusion.

'As you are aware, Inspector, it is a tendency, amongst the criminal element, to adopt an alias. You can imagine, therefore, my amazed satisfaction when, on examining the birth certificate of Nellie McCumber, I found the name of Ryson Douglas listed as being her father!'

Neither Hopkins nor Mrs McCumber could suppress their emotions for a moment longer.

'Good heavens, Holmes!' Hopkins exclaimed. 'That was the name of our chief suspect in the counterfeit case!'

'Stop, please Mr Holmes,' Mrs McCumber pleaded through her vehement sobbing. 'Let me explain the rest to my daughter, and why she never knew that the late Captain John Dyson was her real father.'

'By all means, madam. You still have much to explain to us all,' Holmes announced with a dramatic wave of his hand in her direction.

The poor woman had, by this time, moved towards her daughter, and placed her arm comfortingly around her shoulders.

'Before you judge me adversely,' she began. 'I must explain to you the nature of my relationship with both the man you thought was your father, and the man who truly was. Mr McCumber died at a tragically young age, it is true, and suffered much with illness before he passed away. Yet even before he was stricken down he had never treated me kindly. He drank far more than was good for him, and whenever the devil alcohol was in him his treatment of me worsened still. He was a loud, vile, bully of a man who quite often dealt violently with me, if the mood was upon him. As his health deteriorated, so too did his treatment of me.

'John Dyson, by which name I knew him then, was a different breed of man. Tall, strong and handsome, he was every inch the dashing, seafaring man of romantic fiction. I beseech you to believe that at that time I had no knowledge of his criminal activities. I met him several times, merely by chance, down by the harbour, each meeting lasting longer as we grew to know each other more. He was so romantic, and before long, we fell deeply in love.'

At this I heard Holmes softly grind his teeth, but out of sympathy for the distressed woman, he managed to suppress his impatience.

'By the time of Mr McCumber's death you had already been conceived, and for your own sake, I decided to keep the truth of your parentage to myself. Of course, after the fire and John's outcasting, this secrecy became still more important to your well being. Despite his injuries, and terrible deformities, my love for him was still alive, and I alone could not desert him.

'Then the truth about the money came out. It had been in the hold of the 'Sea Lizard' when she went down, yet sealed and secure within oilskin lined lead boxes, and lying in shallow waters. Frustratingly accessible, yes, but only to a fit, healthy, man with eyes. He only wanted the money to make a better life for me and I only wanted it so that I could make a better life for you, dear Nellie.

'That was why he struck that ill-fated deal with the devil himself, Linus Rawlins. He and his 'weasel' already had something of a reputation for various dubious and underhand dealings. In a village as small as ours, even a minor misdemeanour soon attracts some gossip, so out of frustration, and against my better judgement, John went to see him. In exchange for half the proceeds, Rawlins agreed to unload the boxes from the 'Lizard' and to store them in his cellar. Each day when John shuffled pitifully down to the inn, ostensibly for supplies, Rawlins loaded some money into the small cask. As far as the townspeople were concerned his daily trips were to collect food and drink, whereas, in reality, I was supplying him with all his needs.

'My part in all of this was to pass the money on to small shops, making minor purchases with large notes, thereby accumulating legitimate currency. This I was indeed loath to do, but such was my love for John Dyson that I would deny him nothing. I began by visiting shops in large local towns, such as Ashford and Canterbury. After a time, however, when there was still plenty of counterfeit money to unload, I realized that the large metropolis of London was a far safer option.

'It was during one of these trips that Nellie, in all innocence, whilst out on a walk noticed some money fall from the cask while John was making his way back up the hill. When Rawlins heard of this he was resolved to do away with my Nellie, in case she told of what she had seen, something she would never do. Yet to his evil, greedy mind she was a threat to his fortune and had to die. It was then that I decided to tell John that he was Nellie's father, and begged him not to let Rawlins kill her. Once the initial shock of this discovery was past, he embraced the idea of having a daughter and warned Rawlins that he would go to the police if he even went near her.

'If only I had not gone to London for that one last trip, John would still have been alive. Unfortunately John wanted me to go one last time. He decided to let Rawlins have the rest of the money, and I was to change as much as I could so that the three of us could afford to move from Broadsea and set up a home together in another part of the country. That was why I was away for so much longer than on previous trips. Even the extra money John tried to bribe him with was not enough to placate that evil man. My dearest John died trying to save his daughter, and thanks to you Mr Holmes, in a way he succeeded.'

By the time she had finished, both mother and daughter were distraught with their mutual grief.

'Watson!' Holmes directed me to minister to them. I managed to get them to swallow some brandy, and to lie down for a few minutes in Nellie's room.

'Quickly, Watson,' Holmes whispered urgently. 'Get our things and come. Our train leaves in fifteen minutes!'

'Should we not wait to make our

farewells?' I asked.

'That, old friend, is precisely what I am trying to avoid. I think I have been witness to enough display of emotion for one day.'

Such was Holmes's desire for haste in our departure, that even Hopkins had to run after us as we made our way up the hill towards the station.

He grasped Holmes firmly by the hand. 'Mr Holmes, once again I find myself in your debt. You have given me a case that would pass a conviction in any court in the land, and closed the file on another.'

'Inspector, you are in danger of becoming my only source of gainful employment. Rest assured, any summons from you will be met by a prompt response from us. Come Watson, if our train schedule is true then we may have time to visit a small bistro around the corner from Victoria that might be persuaded to serve us a late supper, and a well earned cognac and cigar!'

The Old Grey Horse

It was a particularly tempestuous evening in early March that found Sherlock Holmes and I sharing the view of Baker Street from our large bay window.

A coarse rain was being driven against our glass by a typically strong, westerly March wind and those passers-by foolhardy enough to venture out into the eye of the storm were being blown along as if they were so many large pieces of street litter.

'Ha!' Holmes suddenly exclaimed, 'It must be an errand of great importance that brings those dank and bedraggled creatures onto the street this night, eh, Watson?'

'Indeed, it must be Holmes and none more so than that poor fool pushing his way forward on our side of the street, down there to the Marylebone end,' I pointed out. 'He appears to be searching for a particular address.'

Before I had finished speaking, Holmes had turned suddenly away and began dressing for the harsh conditions outside. In answer to my astonished look, Holmes explained.

'Whilst you have busied yourself at your practice these past few days, I am glad to report that I have not been entirely idle myself. Indeed, Watson, I have been of some small assistance to our old friend Lestrade in the matter of some, apparently connected, jewellery thefts. Though the conclusion of this matter is, in my estimation, some way off, Lestrade has engaged a valuable informer whom he promised, would come to me with some vital information this very evening.

'I trust you will be able to amuse yourself for the next twelve hours or so, for, unless I am very much mistaken, that poor bedraggled fellow you most astutely observed, is this same man and, therefore, I must leave at once.'

To my astonishment, as he finished speaking, we could hear a loud knocking at the street door below and, without waiting for a summons from Mrs

Hudson, Holmes was gone.

For a few moments I stayed by the window and watched Holmes's and Lestrade's informer hasten down the road through the thin veil of rain. Then with a shiver I turned away and took to my chair by the fire, well fortified with a glass of brandy and a cigar.

I realized, after a few reflective moments, that it would be folly to speculate as to Holmes's movements. From past experience I knew that once on a scent Holmes could disappear for days on end, rather than merely hours. His energy, at times like this, was boundless and his self-deprivation of both rest and sustenance sometimes bordered on the dangerous. He would then return at last, usually satisfied with his efforts, but always totally spent.

I was sure such would be the case in this instance, and resolved, before turning in, to busy myself the following day at my surgery once again and extract more information from Holmes in the evening, should he have returned by then.

I returned to Baker Street at six o'clock

the following evening, but was disgruntled to hear from Mrs Hudson that I was to partake of a lonely supper and that no word had been received from Holmes all day.

I amused myself for the rest of that evening by reading an examination of the life and career of General Gordon, by the light of the fire. At approximately half-past-ten, when my eyes were starting to close and I was ready to retire, I became aware of a commotion emanating from the hall below. I went to the landing and called down to Mrs Hudson.

'Is there some news of Mr Holmes, Mrs Hudson?'

'No, Doctor, but there is a gentleman here to see him, he says he has most urgent business with him and will not be put off.'

'Indeed, then show him up immediately if you please,' I replied, surprised at the tingle of excitement the prospect of this development had given me.

I waited by the door of our sitting-room to show my visitor through and found myself confronted by one of the largest individuals I had ever encountered. He stood at a height of at least six foot four, and was broad to boot. Yet there was something in his manner, which belied his appearance, and suggested that he posed no physical threat. I therefore introduced myself and did not hesitate in showing him to our visitor's chair by the fire.

Despite his size, a more pathetic, bedraggled figure you could not find. There had been no respite in the inclement weather, so obviously he was soaking wet, the front of his uncovered hair dripping in cascades down his face and his clothes were old and threadbare. This then was Benjamin Matthews.

I attempted to alleviate some of his discomfort by bringing him a towel and a warming drink.

'I apologise for my colleague Mr Holmes's absence, but he is engaged on a case at present, which demands all of his time,' I began.

'Not at all. I am grateful for your seeing me at this late hour and at such short notice.' When he spoke there was no mistaking his broad Yorkshire accent, which surprised me somewhat, for he seemed ill able to afford a journey of such a distance merely for a consultation. 'The fact that you accompany and most ably assist Mr Holmes in most of his cases is well known and I have every confidence that you will convey my story to him as soon as you are able. In the meantime any advice you might give me would be most appreciated.'

I bowed slightly in gratitude and took out my pencil and notebook.

'Please proceed.'

'Well sir, to begin with, my story is as brief as it is bizarre.'

'Indeed,' I said with a smile, 'well that will certainly attract Mr Holmes's immediate interest, for his taste tends towards the unusual.'

'That my tale is, but I must be brief, for I will be missed before too long. As you can see from my clothes, I am at present embarrassed financially, and my recent search for accommodation, close to central London, and at a cheap price, proved almost impossible.

'However, two weeks ago, during a long trek which took me northward from Ladbroke Grove into Kilburn Lane, I came upon a curious little side turning called, inappropriately, Regent Street. I say inappropriately because this little road could not be more different from its more famous namesake, being little more than one hundred yards in length and containing very few buildings.

'The side walls of the Kilburn Lane facing premises take up a large section as you enter the street and apart from a couple of warehouses, there are no other buildings save one. This is the most curious of all, being one of the largest and most impressive looking public houses I have yet to see, but it stuck out like a sore thumb in such a tiny road.

'I have come to you, however, because its location and appearance are not the only thing that is unusual about the 'Old Grey Horse', that's the name of the place. Despite its size and the fact that there were no other residents, the landlord and his lady seemed very reluctant to accept my custom. I was not to be put off, however, and even offered my services as an odd job man and cleaner for very nominal pay and lodgings. I must say at this point that if there is a more miserable and unpleasant couple than Jonathan and Agnes Blackwood, I have yet to meet them. In my two weeks there I have yet to receive a pleasant or friendly word from either of them. They really are made for each other, being the same size and build, large, ruddy and untidy.

'The room I was given is in the attic and, like the rest of the building, is in a bad state of repair, so as well as being small and uncomfortable, my room is exceedingly damp. Yet, despite it being almost uninhabitable, the Blackwoods demanded that I keep to my room for several hours each day. The curious thing is that the times when they want me to take to my room vary from day to day and in length: two hours one day, six the next. The times of my duties vary as well, and if I wish to go out they always demand that I return through a side door.'

'A most miserable existence, Mr Matthews, I must say, and it is appalling that these Blackwoods should take such advantage of your present financial plight. Yet you have still to mention the reason for your consultation.'

'I believe, Doctor Watson, that some sinister, criminal activity is in operation at the 'Old Grey Horse'. Why else should the Blackwoods keep me to my room for all that time and require my entrance through the side door? What other reason can there be for the lack of other residents? Not only that, but the main bar is never used by more than five or six regulars. Every evening at seven o'clock the same men take up their positions, always leaving together, then separating upon reaching Kilburn Lane. This much, at least, I can see from my small attic window.

'There is another oddity that I should mention at this juncture. On the rare occasions that my duties compel me to enter the saloon bar, I have observed that ale is never served. It is strange for, as you know, the staple drink in any bar is ale and yet I have never even heard it being ordered. I cannot be sure, of course, but I am almost certain that no dray has ventured near the place during the two weeks that I have been in residence.'

'I agree, most curious circumstances, but none that point directly to a crime,' I said, certainly interested in the strange activities at the public house, yet still unconvinced that any of these warranted the intervention of Sherlock Holmes.

'Then consider this,' Matthews continued, obviously agitated, 'despite all my industry, the Blackwoods are always critical of my efforts. This despite their own standards of cleanliness leaving a lot to be desired, as does their general appearance. They are most particular when it comes to my cleaning; neither corner nor recess is excluded from their scrutiny, save the cellars. For some reason they are strictly forbidden to me. Indeed, the strength of the door and the standard of the locks indicate the presence of something other than barrels of beer and bottles of wine. Yet, on three occasions, in the early hours of the morning, when I have chanced to be sleeping lightly, I have been awakened by a strange creaking noise — perhaps that of unoiled door hinges. Not from the inner cellar door, you understand, but, I am convinced, from the double outer door in the paving, through which beer is normally delivered. But at the dead of night!'

'Again, most unusual Mr Matthews. I am beginning to appreciate your misgivings, I must confess.' As I said this I was aware of Matthews glancing agitatedly at the clock and then he rose with a jolt.

'I must leave now, for fear of arousing their curiosity. Before taking my leave, however, I must tell you that the Blackwoods' behaviour, of late, has become increasingly hostile and menacing towards me, almost as if they know of my suspicions. I would ask you to plead with Mr Holmes on my behalf, and request his early intervention.'

'You are in fear of your life then?' I asked solemnly.

'Indeed I am, Doctor Watson, but not just of my own. I fear the Blackwoods' activities are of a most dark and sinister nature. For on the occasions when I have heard the outer cellar doors opened, a few moments later these sounds have been proceeded by the cries and wailing of what sounded like young children.'

'Children!' I cried in horror. 'Are you certain of this?'

'As sure as I can be from that distance, the attic to the cellar is some way apart in so large a building, yet I cannot attribute these sounds to any other source.'

'Fighting cats?' I suggested.

'That's exactly the theory put forward by the police when I told them my story. I am sure my appearance prompted their rude and dismissive attitude towards me. I am convinced, however, that the source of these sounds was human and not feline.'

'Mr Matthews, if you are in fear of your life why do you not depart from your sinister lodgings?'

'There are two reasons for my remaining. I live in hope that I may locate these children and perhaps, help them escape or aid them in some way. Also, from my position inside the building I may prove of assistance to any action you or Mr Holmes may choose to take.'

'You are a brave and honourable fellow, but alas Mr Holmes may not return to these rooms for days yet, and even then I can offer no guarantee that he will take up your case. However, I will help in any way I can and between us, with resolve, we may yet bring the Blackwoods to task. I suggest you return to your room immediately and tomorrow afternoon I will come, posing as a customer to see what can be learned from the outside.'

We shook hands and Matthews raced down the stairs and through the front door in a few bounds.

After a fitful night's sleep, I ate a light breakfast before taking up my vigil by the window in the faint hope of Holmes returning before I left for the 'Old Grey Horse'.

By lunchtime it was apparent that this hope was in vain, so without further ado I departed for Kilburn Lane.

I alighted from my cab some two hundred yards from Regent Street not wanting to create any suspicion, a cab being an unlikely mode of transport for a patron of that particular establishment.

As I walked slowly towards my destination, I became immediately aware of my dismal surroundings.

Each side of the narrow thoroughfare was lined by small terraced buildings in a poor state of repair. Small, commercial premises, which were hardly flourishing businesses were at street level, whilst above were squalid little flats with filthy windows, each sill full of drying clothes which seemed hardly any cleaner than their surroundings.

Matthews had been most accurate in his description of Regent Street and its layout, except, perhaps, the incongruity of the presence of the 'Old Grey Horse'. Despite its obvious decay, it was still an imposing building and heightened my sense of foreboding. I decided, however, to put a brave face on it, and throwing away the remnants of my cigarette, strode purposefully through the door of the lounge bar. My gait did not falter as I approached the bar.

'Good afternoon landlord!' I boomed, in as cheery a voice as I could muster. 'A pint of your best stout and a slice of meat pie if you please.'

My bluff was called immediately, for the response was as dour and miserable as the man who offered it.

I will not be colouring the truth if I say Jonathan Blackwood presented one of the most unedifying visions I have yet beheld. A man of his size and build should, by rights, have been a most imposing figure, however, so slothful was he in the manner in which he held himself, that he resembled a huge sack of potatoes tied together in the middle. His evil-smelling and discoloured shirt spilled over his worn leather belt and he wore no jacket. His hair had not been washed, much less cut, in what looked like months. He was unshaven and he leaned forward on the bar with the dog-end of a cheap cigar stuck to his bottom lip.

'Ain't got none,' he said, barely glancing at me from the corner of one eye. He then revealed a few blackened teeth by way of a half grimace and half sarcastic smile.

Two strange guttural sounds announced the amusement of one of the equally unbeguiling regulars I now noticed scattered around the lounge. There was something in the manner of this group of singularly unattractive individuals that suggested they shared a common cause. Though I could only guess at the true nature of this. Just the thought of the menace in their eyes, and the recollection of Matthew's narrative, made me shudder and almost balk at proceeding any further.

However, I remembered I was representing Holmes, and Matthews was relying on my assistance, so, once again I attempted to force Blackwood's hand.

'Well then, perhaps a pint of ale, if nothing else is available,' I suggested cheerfully.

Blackwood's manner and expression showed no change; only the cigar fell from his lips onto the bar and this he brushed away with the blackened sleeve of his shirt.

'Ain't got much of nothing 'ave I. Not your lucky day.'

'Try the 'Plough' on the corner,' a voice from the window drawled.

I glanced in its direction and immediately regretted having done so, for there sat Albert Collins, a notorious safe breaker, whose incarceration Holmes and I had brought about some five years previously. I felt myself flush and hoped his memory was inferior to mine. I turned about immediately and made for the door.

'Yes, perhaps I will,' I mumbled as I made my way outside.

The fresh March air immediately cooled my head and I just stood there smoking a cigarette while I collected my thoughts and decided on my best course of action. Thankfully no-one had, so far, followed me through the door. I decided to return to Baker Street and await the long overdue return of Sherlock Holmes. I was debating between Ladbroke Grove and Kilburn Lane as the most likely place to locate a cab, when I noticed a small alley which ran between the back yards of the Kilburn Lane shops and the side wall of the 'Old Grey Horse'.

I noticed the cellar doors set in the pavement and, remembering Matthews's narrative, decided to examine them more closely. I realized that at night, due to the narrowness of the alley, they would be virtually invisible from Regent Street, much less Kilburn Lane. So my mind turned towards the flats above the back of the shops. Even from the vantage of their height, the high walls at the rear of each yard obscured the cellar doors. They were ideal for any nocturnal criminal activity.

Before turning for home, one fanciful hope that the doors had been left unsecured occurred to me. I crawled down and began fingering their edges. Just then I noticed Matthews standing by the side entrance, but his gestures, and calls were not those of greeting, they were a warning! Too late I heard footsteps behind me, and in an instant my head reverberated with a deadening crash. For a moment a sharp light ignited my eyes and I remember raising my hands to my head in an effort to suppress the agony. Then, complete oblivion . . .

My recollection of awakening is most vague. I had, as I learned later, been unconscious for at least twelve hours and, on opening my eyes, was painfully aware of the most terrible throbbing pain in my head and ringing in my ears.

I can then recall constant, violent tremors of shivering. A terrible damp chill ran through me and caused, what seemed to be, every muscle in my body to ache most acutely. My leg, of course, was causing me a greater discomfort than I had experienced in some years. My medical knowledge told me that this unhealthy state could not continue for much longer before serious damage was caused.

I tried to think coherently and soon realized that any escape attempt I was going to make would have to be made before my remaining strength ebbed away from me. Clearly this would be no easy task, as both wrists were most securely tied together with a rough cord and I was tightly gagged.

Fortunately for me at that moment the thought of Holmes coping in this situation jolted me out of a stupor of lethargy and self-pity, which, I fear, I had been slowly sinking into. Even unconsciousness was beginning to seem preferable to the pain and discomfort I was experiencing.

Holmes's fervent mind would already have seized upon a method of escape, whilst I had still to establish my location. I let my eyes adjust to the darkness and slowly realized that there was little enough, in the room, for them to take in. My back was propped against a damp brick wall and I was facing another, barely fifteen feet away. Ten feet to my right was another large wall, whilst to my left I began to define the shape of an occasional cask or two.

I was indeed in an ill-stocked and redundant beer cellar and I was in little doubt that it was beneath the 'Old Grey Horse'. It was obvious that Albert Collins's memory had not failed him after all. That being the case, my predicament was, indeed, of a most serious nature, for Collins had always played a dangerous game and I could be sure that his acquaintances were no less unsavoury.

My frantic efforts at loosening my bonds drew no response from the tough cord; however, when I was almost resigned to my fate, I thought I detected a slight movement in the dark corner to my right. My initial thoughts were of rats and then even hallucinations, but gradually, and to my great surprise, I made out the indistinct outline of a prostrate human form.

A slow laborious kind of snake-like movement, using my elbows and knees, brought me a few feet closer to my fellow occupant and, to my dismay, I found Matthews bound and gagged in a like position to myself. From his lack of recognition and his slumped position I could tell he had suffered physical abuse I had so far escaped. It was only afterwards that I saw his numerous facial scrapes and bruises.

Nonetheless, I could see the advantage of the two of us working together at loosening our bonds, over my lone, vain attempts. With this in mind, I began gesticulating with my eyes and head in the hope that he might recognise what I required of him. After a few moments he realized my intent and with great difficulty began turning his back towards me. In this position we might work in unison at locating any weakness in the knots, encumbered though we were.

At one stage, I thought I had discovered a flaw in Matthew's binding and in my determination to pursue this, overstretched somewhat, and fell over onto one side. Now all hope was lost for, trussed up as I was, I had no means of leverage to right myself once more. I felt as helpless and awkward as a freshly landed trout.

It was at that precise moment that we both caught our breath, for there, surely, coming from above, was the sound of someone handling the large padlock that secured the outer cellar door. Once more my body trembled violently, though this time it was not due to the damp or cold. I must confess that this was pure fear, for I thought this must be Blackwood and his gang coming down to 'finish' the two of us off once and for all.

After a few moments we heard the padlock being unlocked and slowly the doors were opened. The pale light of a street lamp sent a weak silhouette of a figure peering down from the street above. Surely it was not Collins or Blackwood, but it was decidedly familiar . . .

'My dear Watson, are you alright!' To my great surprise and eternal relief Sherlock Holmes was climbing hurriedly down into the cellar.

Too often in my journals I have reflected on my companion's inability to lower his mask of cold, hard logic. The machine-like workings of his mind, his complete absorption in his work at the expense of any affection or warmth. I lay there on the cellar floor, my inaptitude and clumsiness exposed to him, expecting the inevitable ridicule and scorn my predicament would surely warrant.

However, to my surprise, neither of these was evident in Holmes's voice or countenance. Indeed he displayed great sympathy and kindness as he gently undid our bonds and helped us to our feet.

'You have done remarkably well, Watson, against impossible odds. I can only apologise that my own failure in concluding this case earlier has resulted in your capture. The informer of that fool

Lestrade was of no use to me at all and led me a merry dance these last two days. But, more in the cab.' Holmes finished with his kindest of smiles as he then proceeded to assist both Matthews and myself through the cellar door and to freedom.

Once the cab was well underway, I became aware that we were not proceeding by the shortest route to Baker Street. When I queried this, Holmes replied;

'It will not be many hours before your escape is discovered. Obviously, when it is and knowing your identity as they do, they will soon recognise who perpetrated it and realize that their game is up. It is essential, therefore, that we option reinforcements from Scotland Yard and round up this despicable gang before they make good their escape.'

'As usual, Holmes, and despite my own personal involvement in this case in your absence, you seem to know much more about what's going on than I do. Yet I fail to see how this can be so,' I queried.

'Ah, but you see I have an unfair advantage over you, Watson, for I have been involved in this case for many weeks now. It was mere chance that led you onto the very road I have been searching for for so long. It will be some while before we reach the 'Yard', therefore, before you explain your involvement in this matter, please allow me to fill in a few of my own sketchy details, and you can fill in the gaps.'

'Agreed!' I exclaimed, knowing I had certain knowledge to which Holmes could have had no access. I must admit I was still in some physical discomfort following my ordeal, as I am sure Matthews was also, but my new enthusiasm for Holmes's narrative and my excitement at the prospect of the coming adventure overshadowed these considerations. Holmes was aware of this, however.

'I fear I am being most thoughtless, Watson, and am running ahead of myself as usual, at your expense. Surely you are in no condition to embark on any fresh adventures. I should instruct the driver to divert to Baker Street before proceeding to Scotland Yard. You and Matthews are in need of care.'

'You shall do no such thing!' I protested, 'Whilst I agree Matthews here needs attention and can carry on to Baker Street, I would feel thwarted if I were not involved in the conclusion of this affair.'

'Watson! The very words I was hoping to hear. If you are sure you are well enough, of course you will be invaluable at my side, as always.' He lit a cigarette, at this moment, and turned to Matthews.

'I will begin with your companion here, whom I presume is our, or rather your, client.'

'A moment, if you please, Mr Holmes,' Matthews quietly interrupted, 'whilst I appreciate your concern at my condition, I feel my time will be better served with you at the 'Old Grey Horse' as opposed to languishing in your rooms at Baker Street. I still hold my key to the side-door and my knowledge of the layout of the rooms will, I am sure, prove of value in the dark.'

Holmes looked long and hard at Matthews whilst smoking his cigarette.

'My wounds are purely superficial, I assure you,' Matthews added hopefully.

‘A most resolute fellow, your Mr Matthews, eh, Watson? Let me see . . . from Yorkshire, obviously from your accent. A hard-working farmer for many years, then finally, all your labour began to bear fruit and you became quite a wealthy man. Wealthy enough to employ others to carry out your work whilst you became quite the landed gentry. Wealth and success were yours. A charming young wife added to your happiness, but then, I fear, tragedy struck, in the form of a fire. I believe a fire which not only destroyed your farm but your wife also.

‘So, homeless, penniless and alone, you journeyed to London hopefully to start a new life and regain your lost wealth. With this in view you began a search for accommodation, as close to central London as possible, where the best opportunities may be found, yet affordable within your, now, most limited means. The ‘Old Grey Horse’ seemed to fill those requirements, and there you were employed in the most servile of tasks earning a pittance and a bed. Unpleasant and uncomfortable as this was, all was relatively well, until certain aspects of your employers' behaviour, manner, and indeed various unsavoury occurrences, led you to believe that something strange was afoot. Hence your visit to Baker Street and your consultation with my colleague here, Doctor Watson!'

I was agog, I must confess, used as I was to my friend's amazing faculties for observation and deduction, his knowledge of Matthews's past verged almost on the uncanny. Though, of course, if I had put forward this conjecture, I would surely have incurred his extreme impatience, so assertive was he on the fact that his was a cold-blooded scientific study. At the same time, I was annoyed with myself for not seeing what Holmes had seen. In so short a time in Matthews's company, his knowledge of him was so much greater, than my own. No doubt sensing my annoyance and curiosity, and being aware that he was about to be bombarded with questions, Holmes quickly continued. He put his finger to his lips and smiled . . .

'My dear Watson, before I answer all your questions, though, I must confess, that knowing my methods as you do, most of my observations are straight forward and should be obvious, allow me to complete the full circle in this extraordinary ring of circumstances.

'As you know, Watson, for some time I have been engaged in the services of Scotland Yard, who have found themselves in some difficulty for a period, regarding a veritable plethora of jewellery thefts. As you are undoubtedly aware, this type of investigation is not normally to my taste, but on this occasion one or two most singular details appealed to me and, indeed, of late we have been making some progress. However, Lestrade's informer, whom you observed in the rain the other evening, proved of no worth at all and I returned home to Baker Street with the problem still weighing heavily upon me. Upon my return, Mrs Hudson informed me of your nocturnal visitor and of your agitated departure the following afternoon. Eventually, with Mrs Hudson's assistance, I located the driver who had deposited you in Kilburn Lane. It was fortunate for you that the torrent of the other evening was replaced with a mild spell of weather. Therefore, traces of your usual tobacco ash, from Bradley's of Oxford Street I believe, were still visible on the paving.

'I found some on the corner with Regent Street and then a most crudely outed cigarette end outside the entrance of the 'Old Grey Horse', indicating that you were indeed, most agitated. Another deposited close by, with very little indication of burning, showed you had lit up again, quickly, upon your return to the street outside. Then I found still more ash on the corner with the alley to the side of the building, which led me to the cellar door and still more ash. I shuddered at the thought of what I might encounter when I noticed the congealed scraping of blood upon the door's edge, but thankfully those fears were unfounded.'

As he said this, Holmes patted my arm affectionately and smiled. I looked at him and smiled back. Rarely in our association had he showed me any affection or warmth and I often thought he just saw me as a part of the furniture, but I saw a glimpse of Holmes's real feelings towards me which made up for the sarcastic and belittling comments he occasionally made.

'Holmes, wonderful though this explanation of how you discovered us is, you have still made no mention of the details of the case that so appealed to you and how they are connected with the predicament you saved us from.'

'Nor how you acquired such detailed knowledge of my earlier life. On this subject, I am sure I have so far, indulged nothing,' Matthews added.

'That much is simple enough; I acquired such knowledge from your appearance, more specifically your hands. Now, come, Watson, sit next to me and observe our friend as I have done. Then put my methods to work.'

I humbly obliged, but learned little more, save Holmes's deduction of the fire, for around Matthews's ear, I observed, for the first time, a large ugly burn scar. As to the rest, well, I had to confess to seeing nothing more.

'If you observe the palms of the hands more closely, you will notice some unusual calluses.' Holmes began reverting, unfortunately, to a more condescending tone. 'These indicate to me a period of hard labour with a shovel or hoe. The ruddiness of complexion and the place of origin, Yorkshire, one of our great agricultural counties, are all evidence that point immediately to farming.'

Suddenly, Holmes slid from his seat and, crouching on the floor of the cab, held up one of Matthews's hands for my examination.

'With your permission, Mr Matthews?' Matthews just shrugged vacantly as Holmes continued. 'Notice here, however, and here, how the wounds have been allowed to heal. This proves, beyond doubt, that, for a period before tragedy struck, Matthews's situation had improved enough for him to designate the more menial tasks to his subordinates. Further evidence of this new-found affluence is to be found in Matthews's attire. I immediately recognised the style and cut of his shirt as being hand made by Gieves and Hawkes, for example, a make seldom found on the backs of the less well off. The fact that it is not yet threadbare, but is badly worn, confirms that his period of impoverishment has been a brief one.' Since he was still holding Matthews's wrist, Holmes continued to examine his hand while Matthews and I sat dumbstruck by the dexterity of Holmes's mind and his power of observation.

'Before I resume my seat, examine the wedding ring, Watson. My assertion that Matthews's marriage was a recent one is confirmed by its condition. Not a blemish or scratch is evident, proving that the marriage took place at a time when it was unnecessary for Matthews to do his own labouring. Traces of harsh cleaning agents under and around the nails point to the present menial tasks he has had to undertake.'

As he resumed his seat, finally releasing Matthews's wrist, Holmes answered my one remaining question.

'As to the age of the wife, that is a supposition based on the faintest of remaining traces of black colouring around the roots of Matthews's hair. Why else should a man in his position bother himself with such vanities, unless he was attempting to impress a younger woman?'

Matthews reddened slightly as he then confirmed that each of Holmes's deductions had been correct down to the smallest detail. At this Holmes sat back contentedly trying to suppress a brief smile.

I added fuel to the fire of my friend's conceit by expressing my heartfelt admiration at his venerable feat of deduction, based on the frailest of detail, frail, at least, to an ordinary mortal.

Holmes, however, waved this aside, 'Watson, please, let us not become too self-congratulatory for our real work has yet to begin, let alone been satisfactorily completed. Now to return to these remarkable jewellery thefts I referred to before. I mentioned two facts that raised an ordinary succession of robberies from the routine and elevated them to a most extraordinary level. As you well know, Watson, to attract my attention, any case or problem requires some singular or bizarre aspect that inevitably baffles the regular law enforcement agencies. In this case, our old friend Lestrade.

‘In each case the only obvious means of access to the property were the tiniest of windows, usually ground-floor larder windows. The main doors and larger windows were always found to be intact. Even my own most thorough examination found no other signs of entry. On two occasions, I discovered traces of the smallest of footprints, in one case on the ground below the window, in the other on the window sill itself. Both suggest the use of children, probably street arabs who would not be missed.

‘The other point which attracted me was the remarkable ability of the safe-cracker employed on each job. Obviously, upon gaining access our tiny intruder opened the front door and allowed in, unless I am very much mistaken, Albert Collins!’

‘Why the very man whom I am sure gave my game away at the ‘Old Grey Horse’!’ I exclaimed.

Holmes rubbed his hands together at this. ‘All the strands then have been neatly entwined together.’

The remaining minutes of our journey

were taken up by Matthews supplying Holmes with the last few details of his experiences whilst resident at the 'Old Grey Horse'. When Matthews made mention of the strange crying at night, Holmes' mood darkened at once and not a sound passed his lips for the remainder of the journey.

At Scotland Yard, Holmes made short work of raising Lestrade and then insisted that we three went ahead of him, not willing to waste any time while he collected his constables.

'I must say, Holmes, there is an element of risk in this sudden urgency, especially if members of the gang, other than the Blackwoods, are present tonight.'

Holmes contemplated me disdainfully. 'There is certainly an element of truth in what you say, Watson, but I should never forgive myself if any further delay should result in our prey making good their escape. Do not forget, once your absence from the cellar is discovered they will realize their game is up and I shudder to think what retribution might be exacted upon their young helpless captives. This is a most odious and abhorrent business, Watson, and I mean to secure the capture of these villains with all the means in my power.'

'You can rely on me, Holmes, if there is danger afoot; this fire-arm Lestrade gave me will be most useful.'

Holmes barely acknowledged me and sank into the dark forbidding recesses of his thoughts, while we made our way in complete silence.

Holmes bade the driver to stop at the exact spot where I had alighted on my first visit. Despite our determination, caution and surprise were still of the essence.

To our advantage, Regent Street, due partially to its size and lack of use, was ill-lit and with as much speed as our stealth would allow us, we made our way to the door at the side of the 'Old Grey Horse'. With relief we had noted the lack of internal light at any of its windows. Surely this meant that the Blackwoods were asleep, two storeys above, and, therefore we might effect the children's escape prior to Lestrade's arrival, in relative safety.

Matthews led me to the Blackwood's bed chamber, outside which I would stand guard, should they be suddenly aroused. In the meantime, Matthews led Holmes down to the smaller of the cellars in search of the children. For ten full minutes I stood there in the dark, for not even the dimmest of lamps lit the landing in that forbidding establishment. The purpose of our perilous task was almost lost to me during that time, as I became engulfed in the darkness and absolute silence of my strange post.

Then, all was confusion: the clumsiness of Lestrade's arrival at the front of the building surpassed all the levels of stupidity that even he had hitherto attained. The clattering of hooves on the cobbled street below was followed by the ardent efforts of three burly constables in battering down the heavy oak street door, with their bare fists.

I was faced with a difficult choice between holding my post or racing away to the front to facilitate the entry of the constabulary. I had almost decided on the latter, when, to add further to my dilemma, the sound of two shots from a revolver echoed up from the cellars, followed by a heinous cry of pain that pierced the air like a shaft of lightning.

In the end my decision was made for me when the Blackwood's bedroom door was violently flung open, crashing as it did so, against the inner bedroom wall. Revolver cocked and at the ready, I stood face to face with the abhorrent apparition of the despicable Mrs Blackwood. She was indeed as vile to behold as her husband, the more so, perhaps, as she was a woman. Of similar height and shape to Mr Blackwood, her bulk exaggerated still further by the many layers of filthy bed-clothes that she wore. The small oil lamp she held was the only light and produced eerie shadows in the corridor and had a surreal effect upon her ogress-like face.

'So, Albert's old friend, Doctor Watson, has returned to us, Jonathan.' Her voice was surprisingly deep and guttural and it chilled me to the core. As she spoke, her husband appeared wielding a large cudgel.

'Yer interfering devil!' he bellowed and raised his weapon as he shoved his wife out of the way.

Not a moment too soon, my nerve returned and I fired my revolver. The bullet hit the advancing Blackwood in the chest. The cudgel fell from his hand as he made one desperate attempt to grab my neck. I stepped back as he collapsed to the floor. It needed no medical examination to determine that he was dead. The reaction I expected from any spouse at a moment such as this was far removed from Mrs Blackwood's dark nature. No grief or tears, no attempt to comfort her husband, just blind rage, the force of which sent her hurtling towards me, her fists hammering at my chest.

Fortunately, two of Lestrade's constables, whom I later discovered had been let in by Matthews, appeared on the landing and, not without some difficulty, restrained the screaming, demented banshee that was Mrs Blackwood. Once I was certain that she was in safe custody, I raced down to the cellar to discover the cause of the two shots I had heard earlier.

To my immense relief, there, in the damp stone corridor, outside the cellar door, was Inspector Lestrade kneeling beside the prostrate form of Albert Collins. The two bullet holes in his chest adequately answered my query. Lestrade gestured to a door next to that which opened into my erstwhile cell.

'He's in there, Doctor, but be prepared for a bit of a shock,' Lestrade warned me.

I entered a small cellar, identical in all but size to the one in which Matthews and I had been held, and there in the far corner were three small boys being comforted by Sherlock Holmes!

My dismay at their plight, bedraggled and emaciated as they were, was matched by my astonishment at the sight of my friend in such a pose.

'My dear Watson, I see all went well with you. By the sound of the gun shots, I would say you were the more accurate in the despatching of Blackwood than I was with Collins,' Holmes said quickly as he noticed my entrance, obviously trying to detract my attention away from the youngest boy sitting on his knee and another with his skinny arms round his neck. He gently disengaged himself, attempting to appear nonchalant.

'The deranged fool was almost upon me when I fired,' I replied modestly, at which Holmes smiled as he got to his feet.

'Nonetheless, these children undoubtedly have you to thank for their salvation and the clumsy arrival of Lestrade. For I am in little doubt that Collins fully intended to use these innocents as a shield to further his escape, had not the hullabaloo out front drawn his attention for that vital moment.'

'It seems his accomplices were as despicable as Blackwood himself, but who are these children, in heaven's name?' I asked.

'That remains to be established, but unfortunately, even in these enlightened times the streets of London are still full of young vagrants such as these and the three here have been most sorely abused and manipulated. I tell you Watson, I shall not rest until I am sure they are properly reinstated whether with their families or others just as suitable. The effects of the Blackwoods' abuse shall not be long-term, I assure you.'

'Well stated, Mr Holmes.' As he entered the room, Lestrade said this without his usual sneer of cynicism. The two constables who entered with him escorted the children to the carriage outside, with a gentleness that belied their size and bulk. 'They will be given the best of care, I assure you. Upon my word, this case of yours took a turn even you could not have expected.'

'For once I must agree with you, Lestrade, and we have Watson here and his peculiar brand of tobacco to thank for the conclusion. I think you will find the stolen jewellery in the storage box in the corner.'

With that, Holmes turned and swept from the room before Lestrade could waylay him with any further questions.

'Holmes, I must confess to feeling a might uneasy about Matthews, after all it was his unfortunate circumstances that led us to the 'Old Grey Horse' in the first place and once Lestrade has finished taking his evidence, he will have nothing.'

'Not quite nothing. Some of the homes that were robbed belonged to extremely wealthy people, the jewellery being of some considerable value. Therefore, the various individual rewards he will receive should return Matthews to something approaching his original position. Undoubtedly, Lestrade will receive his due credit for the considerable, if uninspired labour which he has put into the case and . . .'

'What of us?' I interrupted mischievously, knowing full well that Holmes's reward was the satisfactory conclusion of the case itself.

'Dinner at Mancini's?' Holmes offered, once we had escaped the dark menacing walls of the 'Old Grey Horse' and breathed in the fresh air once more.

'I should be delighted,' I laughed as we went in search of a hansom.

The Adventure of the Conscientious Constable

Towards the end of a particularly harsh inordinately long winter, I was awakened one morning in early March, by a shaft of sunlight that had penetrated my curtains. Greatly encouraged by this early sign of spring I decided to rise immediately and, despite a chill that was still in the air, take an early morning stroll and return with our morning papers before the remainder of the household had risen.

Holmes had only concluded a long and testing case the day before, and had not returned to our rooms until well after midnight. Therefore, I could not contemplate awaking him at this early hour and so set forth on my own. I lit a cigarette and upon closing the door was immediately struck by the invigorating effect of the early morning air. I decided to extend my walk beyond the newsagents and, only the pangs of hunger some twenty minutes later prompted my return to our rooms.

As I ascended the stairs, it was with some surprise that I detected voices coming from the rooms above, and there, seated at our small table, was Sherlock Holmes, as bright and alert as ever, deep in conversation with a most troubled looking Inspector Lestrade.

By the late '90s the relationship between Holmes and Lestrade had changed somewhat, from their earlier mutual distrust and antagonism. Indeed, from the date of Holmes's unheralded and wonderful deductions which resulted in the exposition, and subsequent arrest, of one Jonas Oldacre, referred to in my narration of the case as the Norwood Builder, Lestrade would often seek his consultation on problems of a particularly vexing nature. No longer hiding his admiration for Holmes's unorthodox methods, Lestrade now enjoyed the successful results that they provided him with.

'Ah, Watson!' Holmes greeted me. 'You are just in time for some most excellent devilled eggs and kidneys which Mrs Hudson has kindly prepared for us at short notice.'

I lost no time in taking my place at the table, and sharing Holmes's enthusiasm for the meal upon it, which made short work of redressing my hunger. Upon observing my questioning glance in Lestrade's direction, and the untouched food on the plate before him, Holmes explained:

'Alas, the dilemma now facing the unhappy Inspector has, somewhat, diminished his appetite, but please finish your coffee and cigarette before we retire from the table. All will then be explained to us by our troubled guest.'

I hurriedly scanned the papers while I concluded my meal, only for Holmes to interrupt my efforts.

'Admirable though your desire for pre-emptive knowledge surely is, I can assure you, Watson, that the delicacy of the matter Lestrade brings before us, and its potentially embarrassing nature, will preclude any mention of it in the press.'

At a gesture from Holmes, we three

moved to the chairs by the fire. Lestrade, pensive and agitated, sat uncomfortably on the edge of his seat. Holmes took to his customary chair, his eyes drooped, almost closed, his finger tips pressed together and, in a state of such total concentration that all matters, save Lestrade's forthcoming narrative, would be excluded. I readied myself to take notes.

During the narrative of earlier cases involving Inspector Lestrade, I have often alluded to his resemblance to a ferret. However, as I sat there, pencil poised to take down his words, I could not help but notice how startling this resemblance really was.

'Gentlemen,' he began. 'I realize how ridiculous it would be of me to request confidentiality, and discretion from either one of you, in view of the loyal service you have given to your country on so many occasions in the past. Indeed, if it was merely my own reputation at stake, in this instance, I would surely have made no mention of it at all. My superiors at the 'Yard' have demanded as much, however, and you must believe me when I say the line of responsibility stretches high above their heads as well.'

These last comments of Lestrade's seemed to irritate Holmes, causing some impatience. Perhaps sensing this, Lestrade cleared his throat, and decided to go to the crux of the matter.

'Now to the known facts, Mr Holmes, without which even you can do very little. My own division have been involved in an investigation of a most delicate nature, but for reasons of national security, each division involved is only allowed a restricted view of the whole picture. We all report to a central agency who, in turn, collate the information, and then report to the relevant government departments.

'Consequently, we will never know the results of our work; whether successful or otherwise. Frustrating though this is, I cannot stress too highly the overall importance of the work, and, therefore, I had to be most selective in my choice of suitable officers. The first name on my list, almost as a matter of course, was Detective Constable Nicholas Parkes, undoubtedly the most accomplished young officer on the force. He has risen to his present rank in just three short years, and his success rate is unprecedented. He has made no secret of the fact that he is a keen devotee of your methods, Mr Holmes, and yet his success is equally due to diligence, and an insatiable appetite for hard work. Incidentally, this appraisal of his work does not come from me, indeed he has only been at the Yard for a fortnight, but from his superiors at two northern constabularies, that proved too small and unchallenging for his talents.'

While Lestrade had been speaking, Holmes had risen, and began collecting the plugs and dottles from his previous day's smokes, which he collected on the top of the mantelpiece and usually employed in his first pipe of the day. Lestrade's unexpectedly early arrival had delayed this process until now. As Holmes lit up his old briar, he could barely suppress his amusement.

'High praise indeed, coming from the equally talented and accomplished Lestrade!' He laughed.

'I can assure you Mr Holmes, I do not exaggerate. In his short time with us he has brought to a successful conclusion no fewer than four cases, the files of which were on the point of being closed. Furthermore, and not withstanding your cynicism, he was immediately put to work on this Government business. He was given the unenviable task of following a certain Theodore Daxer, an agent from Austria, under diplomatic immunity.

'Parkes was only three days into his surveillance when his immediate superior, a Sergeant Gates, reported him as missing, and he has not been seen or heard from since. The current diplomatic turbulence on the Continent is so intense at present, what with alliances being made and broken with alarming frequency, that these foreign agents are playing for very high stakes. Therefore, I have little doubt that Daxer has done away with the unfortunate Parkes, or perhaps worse still, is holding him in an attempt to extract vital information he mistakenly thinks he might hold. Despite all our efforts, and the considerable

Government resources at our disposal, we have had no luck, Mr Holmes, no luck at all.'

'Hence your unsociably early arrival here this morning, presumably on the insistence of your superiors. No doubt they share your conviction that Parkes's disappearance is, somehow, connected to Daxer and his fellow conspirators?' Holmes asked.

'Indeed they do Mr Holmes,' Lestrade replied emphatically.

'Are there no other cases on which he is currently employed, that may have led to his untimely disappearance?' I asked hopefully.

'None whatsoever.' Lestrade replied. 'Each officer chosen for this special force has been withdrawn from all his previous duties.'

'If I am to involve myself with this most singular affair, I shall require a full roster of Parkes's comings and goings over the last forty-eight hours,' Holmes demanded.

'Oh Mr Holmes, if only that were necessary! The irony is that there are none, because Daxer has not left the walls of the Langham Hotel since his arrival in England. We were notified of his imminent arrival by our own agents on the Continent, and he was followed to the Langham directly from the station.

'Since then Parkes has shared a twenty-four-hour surveillance with Detective Constable Benjamin Cryer. The alarm was raised yesterday afternoon, when Parkes failed to relieve Cryer at the appointed time. Cryer is too good an officer to abandon his position; consequently Sergeant Gates was only alerted by Cryer failing to produce his end of shift report. Hence the time lapse between Parkes's disappearance, and my arrival at Baker Street this morning.' Lestrade hesitated before concluding. 'I must admit that we are all very much relying on you, Mr Holmes.'

Holmes gleefully rubbed his hands together as he paced, back and forth, in front of the fire.

'Oh, Watson, this is absolutely priceless!' he exclaimed.

Although more successful at concealing it than my friend, I could not help but share Holmes's obvious delight at the situation. So often in the past Holmes had saved the police from humiliation with his timely interventions, and so often he had denied himself, or been denied, his full and due credit. The crestfallen policeman would now see this as Holmes's ultimate triumph.

'Watson, not only are our colleagues at the 'Yard' bereft of all reason and logic, but now it seems they misplace their officers to boot! I would not miss this for the world!' Holmes proclaimed whilst slapping Lestrade upon his rounded shoulders.

'I suppose I should have expected this kind of reaction from you,' Lestrade responded disconsolately. 'However, I would implore you not to trivialise the situation. There is a lot more at stake here than saving the blushes of Scotland Yard.'

Turning away from Lestrade, Holmes made a great effort at suppressing his amusement. 'No, no, of course not. To trivialise is as great a sin as to exaggerate, especially in advance of the facts. Would Constable Cryer be on duty at the

Langham at this hour? Good, then we shall begin our investigation there,' Holmes announced upon noting Lestrade's affirmation. 'We shall need a cab at once. Mrs Hudson!'

As we approached the Langham, Lestrade once more emphasised the need for discretion, and as a consequence, decided to relieve Cryer from his duty, and send him down to be interviewed by Holmes in the cab.

Even in plain clothes, Cryer's bearing and thick set build made his profession fairly obvious to the trained eye. A pleasant enough young man, in his early thirties, with a mop of wispy dark hair, and a surprisingly soft, modulated tone to his voice.

'Good day gentlemen,' he began, 'Inspector Lestrade has asked me to assist you in your inquiries in any way I can. I shall be only too happy to oblige.'

Ignoring his courtesies, Holmes immediately bombarded the young policeman with a series of brief questions.

'I understand you have not known Parkes for very long, and yet I would hope that an aspiring young detective, like yourself, would have formulated some opinion as to his character and behaviour.'

'Indeed I have, sir. Despite the brevity of our association, any opinion I do have is of a most favourable nature. His past record speaks for itself, and my own first hand knowledge of him has done nothing to discredit or change that. His reliability and dedication are second to none,' Cryer concluded.

'All very commendable and professional viewpoints, yet do you not have instincts of a more personal nature?' Holmes asked.

'Well no, sir.' Here Cryer hesitated for a moment and Holmes glanced quizzically at him from under a raised eyebrow. 'You see,' Cryer continued, 'Parkes is a most unsociable sort of fellow when off duty. Not rude, but distant, almost aloof you might say. For example, occasionally some of the lads take themselves off for a pint or two of ale when our duties, and shifts are completed, to relax together, and help build up the comradeship that is essential to any force. Parkes, however, always makes an excuse, and always has someone to see, somewhere to go. Yet, as far as I know, he has no sweetheart, no family, and only a small room in a lodging house to go home to. There is certainly something odd there, I would say.'

'Would you indeed,' Holmes murmured, pursing his lips with his forefinger, while gazing thoughtfully through the cab window. After a few moments Holmes resumed his questioning.

'What opinion or theory have you formed as to Parkes's nocturnal activities?'

'I know so little of him it is impossible to guess,' Cryer replied.

'You mean he has never referred to the people he is staying with, nor any friends or associates he might have?' Holmes asked.

'Not a word, sir. Like a closed book, he is, totally obsessed with his work to the exclusion of everything else.'

'Highly commendable, no doubt, and yet he sounds almost too good to be true,' was Holmes's surprisingly cynical response. 'I take it he has never been late to a meeting before this, nor missed a duty?'

'Not once, indeed I am convinced that something awful must have overtaken him for it to have occurred on this occasion,' Cryer emphatically replied, then he added thoughtfully: 'Yet Daxer is still to leave his room.'

'Thank you, Constable.' Holmes waved him dismissively from the cab, and then sat deep in thought, his eyes adopting that far away glaze I was so used to seeing at times like these. Indeed, even when Lestrade rejoined us, Holmes seemed as oblivious to his presence as he was to mine.

'I must see a list of Parkes's most recent cases,' Holmes muttered, almost to himself.

'Surely the answer lies with Daxer, and his associates. I do not understand why you should require such a list.' As he asked this, Lestrade shot a questioning glance in my direction, no doubt surprised at Holmes's lack of response to his query. I could merely shrug my shoulders, and remained as puzzled as him. In fact the entire journey back to Baker Street was completed in total silence, save for Lestrade moaning about the traffic, and the endless paperwork waiting for him back at his office. It was only as we pulled up outside 221b once more, that Holmes spoke again.

'I shall also require Parkes's last known address. It is very likely I shall wish to call there within the next few days. Come along, Watson, we have a busy night ahead of us.' Then, without even a nod in Lestrade's direction, Holmes was gone.

Upon reaching our rooms, Holmes immediately went to the mantelpiece where he filled his old clay pipe from his Persian slipper, and sank into his chair with a long sigh.

'There are certain aspects of this case that trouble me, Watson. Even allowing for the current sparseness of information, something far removed from the ongoing theory is constantly nagging at my brain. I cannot yet identify it, and yet . . . ' His words slowly trailed away, and he sank into a deep meditation while drawing heavily on his pipe.

'You are not convinced of Daxer's involvement then?' I ventured to ask, knowing full well the potential dangers involved in interrupting Holmes's chain of thought.

'I must see the list,' Holmes repeated to himself, then glancing briefly towards me, and acknowledging my question, he added: 'I do think it most unlikely. Consider for a moment the type of men we are dealing with here. International agents, playing for extremely high stakes. I am sure that, by now, they are fully aware of the police surveillance, I mean, diligent our officers of the law may be, but subtle they are not! Therefore, Daxer, and his confederates are hardly likely to jeopardise their mission, and draw attention to themselves still further by eliminating a police officer. No, I am sure our search for Detective Constable Parkes must lie in another direction.'

Almost as soon as he had finished speaking a messenger from Scotland Yard arrived bearing a large, buff envelope, announcing it to be for the attention of Mr Sherlock Holmes. Holmes grabbed at it greedily, tore it open, and extracted two large sheets of paper which he sat down with at the table. Having read through them quickly, he then began writing furiously on six separate sheets of note paper. By now I had become aware of the messenger's discomfiture, and drew Holmes's attention to the man's continued presence, in the hope that he would, at least acknowledge him.

'Oh, yes. My thanks to Inspector Lestrade for his promptness, there is no reply. Oh, and ask Mrs Hudson to step up on your way out will you?' He yelled these last few words, as the messenger was already half way down the stairs, and he had returned to his note writing.

Somewhat put out by the nature of Holmes's message, a disgruntled Mrs Hudson appeared in our room to be told she had to despatch the sheets of paper Holmes had been scribbling on immediately. He gave her precise instructions as to the destinations of all six wires.

'Holmes,' I began hesitantly, 'evidently events are unfolding which I cannot even begin to comprehend, and I gather, with some urgency. Yet I have neither seen, nor heard, anything so far which could possibly have prompted them.'

'Events quite often appear to be more dramatic than they really are. I have merely despatched Mrs Hudson with messages to six of Shinwell Johnson's most used haunts. Unless his habits have changed dramatically, since he was last of use to us, he should arrive here before we are ready to retire for the night. Hopefully with enough information to justify my requesting this list.'

'Ah, the list! That has told you something of Parkes's whereabouts then?' I asked.

'Your conjectures are too premature even for me,' Holmes replied. 'However the list has certainly taught me a good deal about Parkes's recent career, and is more relevant than Lestrade's foreign friends at the Langham.'

I should mention here something of the nature of our acquaintance and occasional colleague, Shinwell Johnson. Mr Johnson, known to various intimates as 'Porky', was Sherlock Holmes's door-keeper to the dark, nether regions of the underworld. A twice-convicted criminal himself, Johnson was forever grateful that he had fallen into Holmes's hands, before his descent had become irreversible, and had therby been saved from himself. Though his associates were still, undeniably shady, he was now a friend of the law, and would not hesitate for an instant in answering a call from Sherlock Holmes. On more than one occasion his invaluable information had proved of great value. He was a stocky fellow, round of face, solid of build, and certainly someone you could rely upon, should events take a turn towards a more violent nature. It was certainly no great surprise to find him standing in our rooms at a quarter past the hour of eleven, later that night, just as Holmes had predicted he would be.

Holmes had always claimed that it was an injustice to nature if one differentiated between a Lord of the realm, and a common scullery maid in the way one treated them. True to this side of his nature, Holmes had greeted Johnson as warmly as one would his closest friend, or dearest relation.

'Well, I am glad to see that at least one

of my messages reached its mark, and a welcome sight you are too, Shinwell Johnson! No doubt the warmth of some alcoholic liquid sustenance would not go amiss?' Holmes suggested.

'No indeed, Mister 'olmes, not at all. Evenin' Doctor, ever the gent your friend 'ere.'

'Indeed he is, Mr Johnson.' I replied.

Holmes casually waved Johnson to a seat whilst handing him a large tumbler of whisky, the contents of which Johnson greedily devoured.

'Now I am at your service Mister 'olmes,' Johnson declared while licking his lips longingly. Taking the hint, Holmes readily recharged Johnson's glass, and then placed Lestrade's list in Johnson's vacant hand.

Treating the second glass with greater respect, Johnson only sipped at it occasionally while carefully studying the list. Eventually he declared: 'Well now, a most han'som collection of treasure 'ere, I must say!' Then after a moment's thought, Johnson eyed up Holmes quizzically, and added: ''ere, I 'ope you don't think that I

’ad anything to do with these, if that’s why you brought me ’ere. Even though they collared the lot, you still suspect old ‘Porky’, eh?’

By now Johnson had agitated himself to such an extent that he put his glass down, rose from his chair, and began making for the door. With a leap Holmes straddled the settee, and was able to reach Johnson before his hand had even touched the handle of the door. With his most charming smile and a reassuring pat on the back, Holmes managed to calm Johnson’s fears, and he in turn resumed his seat apologetically.

‘Now to business,’ Holmes began, standing over Johnson with his finger tips pressed together before him. ‘No doubt you will have noticed that in each case the arresting officer in question was the redoubtable Detective Constable Parkes. Now, I am convinced that there must be one factor, other than he, that connects each of the cases. I am hoping that you, with your most singular, and extensive knowledge of such things, can supply me with that connection.’

‘Well I will certainly do me best, Mister ’olmes,’ Johnson replied, taking up the list once more. He read slowly through it once again, only this time we could hear him dismiss certain possibilities as he considered each one in turn. The location of the properties in question; the size, and contents of the haul procured by each thief; the manner of achieving access; even the events leading up to each arrest. Every dismissal saw Johnson dejectedly shake his head, and Holmes’s agitation increase. He began pacing before the fireplace, casting furtive glances towards Johnson every time he went past him.

‘Blimey, Mister ’olmes!’ Johnson suddenly exclaimed. ‘I must be going soft in the ’ead for not realizing it sooner. It must be the fence. I am almost certain that Silas Morrison was the one that moved the stuff every time.’

‘I think I take your meaning,’ Holmes replied. ‘Is there any chance you might know where this individual could be found?’

‘There is a certain establishment in the East End where ’e, and ’is, shall we say, associates meet most evenings. I've been 'ere too long for me own good!' Shinwell suddenly exclaimed leaping from his seat. 'I'll send word to you tomorrow evening, but please, for all our sakes, be careful, and discreet.'

'I can assure you, I am more than adept at blending in,' Holmes replied. 'You will hardly know I am there at all. Goodnight to you, Johnson!'

Johnson doffed his cap to us both, and was gone.

'A most satisfactory conclusion to the day, would you not agree, Watson?' Holmes asked, once the door had closed behind our hastily departing guest.

'Most certainly, although the situation of Constable Parkes seems somewhat darker when seen through our latest discoveries. It would seem that Parkes was closing in on Morrison, and his gang, and he in turn has incommoded Parkes. Or worse perhaps,' I suggested thoughtfully.

Holmes nodded solemnly, and lit his old clay pipe.

'Will you not now retire, Holmes?' I

asked. Then I observed that familiar faraway look come over Holmes's steely grey eyes, and I already knew my answer.

'Best get some sleep, old fellow. An early morning trip to Islington will be the order of the day tomorrow.' He spoke these last words absently, as he sank slowly into his chair. He drew his bony knees up to his chin, and sank into a deep chain of thought by the glowing embers of the dying fire. I shook my head as I made my way slowly, and quietly, to my room knowing full well that, despite his late night vigil, Holmes would seem the fresher of us, come the morning.

To say that my surmise of the previous night was borne out by Holmes's appearance and mood the following morning, would be to understate in the extreme. Unusually, he was most jaunty as our hansom rattled us towards London's more northern suburbs, although he would not be drawn on the subject of Constable Parkes's disappearance, either during our hasty breakfast, or during the course of our journey to Islington.

Although he had kept the nature of our

visit a complete mystery, I was in little doubt that the address Lestrade had furnished us with, in relation to Parkes's lodging house, was our current destination. I could not help noticing that the closer we came to our destination, the more steadily decreased the size and quality of the dwellings we passed. By the time we reached Conway Avenue, they had become dark, gloomy terraced houses, badly kept up, and of miniscule proportions.

'What a ghastly place!' I declared, depressed by our surroundings. Holmes merely grunted as he alighted from the cab and called for the driver to wait for us; we crossed the avenue to number 41. The appearance of the house was certainly no worse than that of its neighbours, indeed, it bore all the signs of having received a coat of paint within the last three years.

There was an immediate response to our knock on the street door, and a particularly short, elderly woman opened it, and greeted us with a cheery smile. Her hair was short, and quite white, while her steel rimmed spectacles seemed to lend a friendly sparkle to her eyes. The grime on her flowered pinafore indicated food preparation.

'Good morning, Mrs Mullins? My name is Sherlock Holmes, and this is my friend, and associate Dr Watson,' Holmes declared in his most charming tone.

'Oh do come in, gentlemen. The inspector did say you might be paying us a call,' Mrs Mullins invited.

The ill-lit hallway we were led into held an awful feeling of dampness, and decay that was all pervading. Yet despite this, what may best be described as squalor, one was equally aware of the diligent efforts of Mrs Mullins, in maintaining a level of cleanliness.

'Before showing you up to Constable Parkes's room, might I offer you both a cup of tea in the scullery? It should not take long for the kettle to boil again,' Mrs Mullins offered.

Displaying a seldom seen consideration and politeness, Holmes nodded his assent, and we were shown into an equally squalid little room, where further signs of Mrs Mullins's simple culinary efforts were evident. Over a surprisingly good, strong cup of tea, Holmes began questioning Mrs Mullins regarding the disappearance of her lodger.

'I am afraid I can add very little to what you already know, Mr Holmes,' Mrs Mullins responded. 'It was only upon the inspector's visit here yesterday evening that I became aware of there being anything amiss myself.'

'Did it not seem strange to you that Parkes should desert his lodgings for three whole days and nights?' Holmes asked.

'No, not at all. You see, when he first came to me Constable Parkes explained that his line of work would require him to work at some very strange hours, sometimes for entire nights. Therefore, I made an exception in his case, and gave him my spare latch key, something I have never done before. He is such a pleasant young man, and after all, he is a policeman.'

'Yes of course, most understandable. Yet how can you be so certain that he never returned to his room, say in the middle of the night? After all I am certain that you retire at a reasonable hour,' Holmes inquired.

'Indeed I do, Mr Holmes,' Mrs Mullins replied. 'Unfortunately, I am a very light sleeper, and I can assure you the sound of the street door opening and closing would awaken me in an instant. I am sure the poor, young man has been at work every night of late.'

Holmes sat in silent thought for a moment, while he considered the landlady's last comment. 'Perhaps an examination of Parkes's bedroom will shed some light on the situation. If, perhaps you would lead the way, Mrs Mullins?' Holmes suggested rising suddenly.

Clearly taken aback by Holmes's abruptness, Mrs Mullins hesitated for a moment before slowly rising and leading us back to the front hall. 'A moment please while I get us an oil lamp to light the way.'

'Most suggestive, would you not say?' Holmes whispered suddenly once Mrs Mullins had moved away. 'Especially when you consider that the duty roster

Lestrade kindly enclosed with the list, clearly shows that Parkes has only been on day duty this past week!'

'I will admit this new information confirms your conjecture that Parkes's disappearance is unconnected to Daxer and his confederates. Officially he was last on night duty before Daxer was even in the country! Though I am at a loss as to what it all means,' I replied, in the certain knowledge that my friend's grasp of the situation was more astute than my own. At that, our hostess reappeared with the necessary illumination and began leading us up quite the narrowest and most precarious staircase I had ever encountered. I admit to feeling much relieved at having safely negotiated it. We were then led down a dark corridor towards the back of the house, and the solitary door at its end.

The single gas light within, gave out barely sufficient light for Holmes's purposes, so he placed the oil lamp strategically on the bedside table, and was then able to begin his research of the room.

The small, uncomfortable looking bed

had been neatly made, and not slept in, Mrs Mullins assured us, for many nights. Save the oil lamp, the table at its side was totally bare, and the room's only chair revealed nothing besides its upholstery, through badly worn patches in its cover.

Holmes grunted irritably at the empty drawers in the tall-boy, and was equally disappointed at the meagre contents of the clothes cupboard, a plain, shabby brown suit. He searched thoroughly in each pocket of this, and finally slammed the cupboard door shut, impatiently.

'Were you not aware that your lodger had removed all his chattels?' Holmes asked, glaring at Mrs Mullins.

'No indeed, sir,' she replied. 'I had no idea. Mind you, sir, I do not think he had that much with him to begin with.'

'More than a single suit I am sure, though.' Then with a finger to his lips, Holmes motioned us both to silence. With his hands on his hips and a single finger from each hand protruding into the top pockets of his waistcoat, Holmes bent his neck, and began surveying the floor, his last recourse for a clue.

He stood in this fashion for a few moments, his intense eyes almost protruding from their sockets, as he continued his search. Suddenly his eyes sparkled briefly, a triumphant smile flashed momentarily, and was then gone. I tried to follow the direction of his gaze, but could see nothing save an old, moth-eaten Chinese rug, surrounded by badly scarred floorboards. A barely audible cry, in fact no more than a brief exhalation of air, announced Holmes's pleasure, and, in an instant, he was laying on his stomach, prostrate on the floor.

Only when his right hand went towards it, did I become aware of a small pile of dust particles, which would surely have been ignored by a lesser mortal. He gathered a small sample of the dust in his left hand, while his right fore-finger sifted through it carefully. Returning the dust to the floor Holmes bent his head upwards to Mrs Mullins.

'Were you aware of your lodger's penchant for expensive cigars? This is the remains of one from the Dutch East

Indies, and is not so easy to obtain.' The tone of this question indicated that any answer would be an irrelevance. Mrs Mullins, obviously surprised at the question, replied nonetheless.

'No, sir. On the rare occasion I saw him smoking, it was usually a cheap cigarette.'

Ignoring the answer, Holmes began getting up once more from the floor when something, even more invisible to me than his previous discovery, apparently caught his eye.

Shuffling across the floor, like some dexterous lizard, he reached his find, and after a brief examination of this, placed it in a small envelope he brought out from his inside breast pocket. He was on his feet again in an instant, passing no comment as to the nature of his discovery and dusted himself down. Hurrying towards the door, he paused briefly to address Mrs Mullins.

'Mrs Mullins, my advice to you would be to advertise a vacancy in your house with immediate effect, for I am now in no doubt that your previous lodger will not be returning. Come, Watson!'

I quietly apologised for my friend's brusqueness and thanked Mrs Mullins for her indulgence, for by now Holmes was already in the street.

'Watson, if Shinwell Johnson proves as reliable tonight as he has been in the past, I think I can look forward to encountering a most singular and brilliant criminal mind before the night is out,' Holmes cheerfully announced once we had rejoined our cab. However, he proved most reticent on the subject for the remainder of our homeward journey, and I felt as shut out from the innermost workings of his mind as ever.

* * *

For an hour upon our return, Holmes entertained us with a most delightful rendition of Beethoven's violin concerto, and he seemed able to shut out all thoughts of Parkes's mysterious disappearance, and the anticipated message from Shinwell Johnson. However as the evening wore on, he became increasingly fretful at Shinwell's lack of communication. He lit cigarette after cigarette, and seemed almost to chew them up as he ceaselessly prowled about our rooms.

'I feel so close to success, and yet, if Johnson fails to locate this fence, Morrison, all my other work, and deductions will become worthless and futile!' Holmes bemoaned.

'I am sure he will not disappoint you. Johnson seems well able to take care of himself, so I am certain no misfortune has overtaken him. If the information is to be had, I am sure he will provide you with it.' My inept attempts at consolation seemed to fall on deaf ears. It was now ten o'clock and there was not much conviction in my voice.

'Yes, but when?!' Holmes exclaimed. He lit another cigarette, and turned to the window from which he gazed intently. He then returned to his chair, crestfallen and apparently exhausted from the expenditure of so much nervous energy. However, within a few minutes he was back on his feet again, rubbing his hands together gleefully. A soft, almost inaudible knock on the front door, had alerted him to the presence of a visitor, before I could even distinguish it. Mrs Hudson having already retired for the night, I was despatched with a wave of the hand to attend the door, while Holmes waited in happy anticipation.

I opened the door to a filthy, dishevelled remnant of a man, unshaven, and reeking of stale beer. An almost lost, and buried instinct within him stirred him to doff his patchwork cap to me, and he attempted a toothless grin as he handed me a small, crumpled piece of paper.

'From Porky,' he croaked.

I slipped the creature a half-crown, and with the treasured piece of paper safely in my hand, I was glad to close the door on so sad a manifestation.

'Quickly, Watson! There is not a moment to be lost.' Holmes called down to me, before I had even glanced at the message myself. I took the stairs two at a stride, and Holmes had snatched the note from my hand before I reached the landing. Bearing the valued note, Holmes disappeared into his room at once, slamming his door shut with a shudder that shook the entire house. So intense was my curiosity that I called out to Holmes through the closed door.

'For reasons best known to yourself, you seem to attach great importance to Johnson's message, yet I fail to see why you must go out at so forsaken an hour. Surely the morning would be time enough.'

Suddenly Holmes's door re-opened, but by only the merest chink, revealing nothing more than the tips of my friend's sharp features.

'Watson, Johnson has risked much in getting this information to me. If I betray him now, and, indeed the citizens of our great city, by shirking my responsibilities due to the lateness of the hour, it would be most reprehensible. Rest assured, all will be explained to you upon my return.'

'You mean I am not to accompany you?!' I cried, aghast at having my services dismissed in such a fashion.

Holmes's answer was the hurried re-closing of his door. When he opened it again, a few moments later, the transformation Holmes had undertaken was the most startling he had yet achieved, even, perhaps, surpassing the gnarled, old book peddler he had used to disguise his dramatic return from death in my narrative of The Empty House.

When I beheld him it was hard to believe that my friend still existed beneath the heavy disguise. As with the book peddler, he had taken two or three inches off his height, by means of a subtle bend of his back and limbs. Clever use of theatrical make-up provided him with three-day facial stubble, and a broken nose. An ugly knife scar on his left cheek, and a set of huge black eyebrows made him appear all the more sinister. His attire, a well worn tweed suit with a gaudy coloured waistcoat, a dusty brown bowler worn askance, and a thin, unlit cigarette protruding from a corner of his mouth, completed the effect. He was, every inch, the vicious criminal down on his luck.

'Gimme' a light mister.' Holmes growled in a broad, gravelly cockney accent.

'Wonderful, my dear Holmes, just wonderful!' I exclaimed, 'For all the world, you will certainly not let Johnson down tonight, if indeed he can recognise you at all!' Then, remembering his callous dismissal of my services, for the coming night's work, I added: 'However, I would have thought my presence tonight might have been of some worth.'

'My dear fellow, of course it would,' Holmes replied, reverting to his gentler tones. 'However, with the best will in the world, you find it somewhat harder than me to blend into the dark and forbidding surroundings I am about to descend into. Shinwell Johnson will be in as much jeopardy as myself, and I should not like to compromise him still further. Besides, should I find myself in difficulties, I am sure Johnson will prove himself a most stalwart ally. I do hope you will still lend me your army revolver?' He asked, with a consolatory pat on my left shoulder.

'Of course I will,' I replied, 'but do take care.'

'Ha! Still the ever watchful Watson. I do not expect to return much before breakfast, so you had best retire. Good night!' That strange, menacing creation of his shot from the room, and I could hear the street door close behind him an instant later.

I had every intention of taking Holmes's most excellent advice, but decided upon one last pipe, and a further chapter of a most rousing account of the American Civil War. I soon realized that any attempt at sleep would surely be futile. This, indeed, proved to be the case, and before long the exploits of General Grant, had paled beside my fears for Holmes, and the outcome of his treacherous night's work.

Five anxious hours later sheer exhaustion slowly dragged my eyelids together, and I was on the verge of losing consciousness when a long, dark shadow standing over me brought me back. Long sinewy fingers were embedded in my left shoulder, prodding it gently, and a familiar voice was speaking to me.

'Come along, Watson, you will do yourself no favours by sleeping here. You really must take to your bed.'

Slowly I raised my head, and Sherlock Holmes was looking down on me, his smile unmistakable even from beneath his most extraordinary disguise. The potential adventures and dangers of the previous five hours suddenly cleared the clouds from my mind, and I was on my feet in an instant.

'Good heavens, Holmes, is it really you!?' I exclaimed. 'Your rendezvous with Shinwell Johnson, did it go well? Please tell me, you are unharmed?'

'All went very well,' Holmes answered calmly. 'Indeed, things went better than my greatest expectations might have allowed. I have concluded a most gratifying night's work. Now, however it is five o'clock in the morning, and my body craves for sleep. Do not worry yourself, I will furnish you with sufficient details for your notes and curiosity later in the day. Besides, you appear to be pretty much done in yourself.'

'Be reasonable Holmes,' I protested. 'The sight of you, standing there in your attire, has dispelled all thoughts of desire for sleep, and I would much rather hear now. My curiosity would render sleep an impossibility, in any event.'

Holmes considered me in silence for a moment, while he began removing his disguise.

'Very well,' he said sharply. 'I suppose your patience, and your concern alone, merit some reward.' Then he added with a short burst of laughter. 'I would have enjoyed having Lestrade here though, while I dispelled his half-baked theories of international espionage. I assume, however, he will hear soon enough.'

Holmes then dashed into his room, and when he finally returned he was dressed in his customary purple dressing-gown, all traces of the unsavoury villain now removed. He lit a cigarette and stood gazing at the dark street below, from our window. The shadow of him, cast by a single gaslight, accentuated the sharpness of his features upon the drapes.

'Watson, as you may have already surmised, I discounted Lestrade's espionage theories quite early on in our investigations,' he began, seating himself cross-legged, upon his chair. 'Although this may have been premature of me, being ignorant, at that time, of so many facts, happily those earlier misgivings have now been dramatically confirmed.

'As you know, the word coincidence has no meaning to me, especially in relation to my work. Therefore, Parkes's disappearance, following the completion of so many identical case investigations, indicated some dark connections.

'Although, until tonight, even I had underestimated the complexity of the matter. Obviously the odious fence, Silas Morrison was the connection, and he, above all others, would have welcomed the removal of Detective Constable Parkes. Thus so far, no doubt, you follow my reasoning, and the necessity for tonight's rendezvous with the underworld.'

'You have made yourself abundantly clear, so far Holmes,' I confirmed.

'Excellent, so now to my discoveries at Mrs Mullins, and how one of them all but saved my life tonight. The cigar ash, as you may have already deduced, indicated that Parkes was in receipt of income from sources other than the Metropolitan Police. His empty wardrobe seemed to indicate that Mrs Mullins's was not his only residence, or perhaps, that he was in the process of moving, without informing his superiors at the 'Yard'. If this was the case, my meeting tonight with Johnson, and Morrison became all the more urgent.'

'I fail to see how either of these discoveries could possibly have led to your life being saved,' I mentioned somewhat cynically.

'I would be very surprised if you could, for it was neither of those. However, if you recall there was another item which I secreted in a small envelope.' As he spoke, he jumped up suddenly, and brought the very same envelope down from the mantelpiece. Offering it to me for examination, I emptied the contents into the palm of my hand, and was not a little disappointed, and surprised, to find nothing more than a single, long strand of bright red hair.

'Now come along, Holmes, how could you possibly believe that this strand of hair saved your life. I see nothing more sinister here than, perhaps evidence of

Parkes having a redheaded paramour.' I laughed at what I believed to be Holmes's exaggeration of the hair's importance. The icy glare, which stole across Holmes's face, proved that my display of amusement had been a mistake. He snatched back the envelope angrily.

'Holmes, I apologise, but perhaps if you were not so inclined to constantly keep information to yourself, these misunderstandings might never occur.'

'Watson, you know I am not, by nature, prone to exaggeration, and if I make a statement, even one as apparently implausible as a strand of hair saving my life, you may be assured that I am stating a plain, and simple fact. However, I must confess that your criticism of my hoarding information is certainly not without foundation. Perhaps if I sketch a brief narrative of all that occurred tonight, things will become much clearer to you.

'The location earmarked by Johnson for tonight's rendezvous, was a gin house situated in one of the most deprived, and decayed sections of East London. Beggars and criminals of every description, male and female, seem to congregate on street corners, or on the steps of every gin house, plying their unholy wares. Indeed, I could not even be sure that my extravagant disguise, was not, somewhat understated.

'Once inside the gin house, having closed the door behind me, the vile stench, of every known human vice and depravity, suddenly seemed to grasp, and engulf me. Stale beer mingled with opium, and dark clouds of cheap tobacco smoke wafted around in huge swells, obscuring the dim gas lights. Old women cackled amongst themselves as they slobbered over their gin, their noise only drowned out by the raucous laughter of some rather large, unsavoury villains supporting themselves upon the bar.

'As you well know, Watson, I am not, as a rule, of a nervous disposition, yet never before have I felt so inclined to retrace my steps, and withdraw. Instead I descended into the mire, and lit my cigarette of shag tobacco. It was only then that I caught sight of Shinwell Johnson. He was, evidently, entertaining a small group of friends, who had convened at the far end of the bar, with some amusing tale. I made my way slowly toward him.

'By pretending to stagger into the side of one of his companions I was able to draw Johnson's attention to my arrival, without betraying him. In consequence, it was made easier for him to identify Morrison to me with equal discretion. Taking my lead, he collaborated with his companion against me, abused me for my clumsiness, shoved me away in Morrison's direction, and singled him out with a deft motion of his head.

'In the furthermost, and darkest corner of the room sat a group of five men cloaked in a film of dense, black smoke, and obviously involved in a most earnest conference. The man in their centre was of a most singular appearance, and the self evident reverence in which the other four held him, left me in little doubt as to his identity.

'Even at this stage of the game I was little aware of how significant my discovery at Mrs Mullins's truly was. The strand of hair had the feel of being part of a wig, no doubt part of Parkes's disguise when operating incognito. As Lestrade attested, Parkes was a devotee of my method, and had often applied it to great success. I was convinced, by now, that Morrison had finally bested him, and felt it incumbent upon me to discover Parkes's true identity and to avenge him.

'To this end, I staggered slowly towards Morrison's table, in my role of the drunk, in the hope of catching Morrison's attention. It was my intention, then, to lure Morrison away from his companions with a story of rich booty to be had. As I drew ever closer, the image of the men in the corner gradually became less obscure, and with a thrill that ran through me, I became aware of my fundamental error, and the true nature of how things stood.

'Watson, I have often underestimated, and berated your earnest literary attempts at illustrating my method, and describing our more singular adventures. However, I must now admit that your writing must certainly evoke some degree of vividness, for there seated before me was Silas Morrison in a perfect facsimile of the disguise I donned when I penetrated the opium den during our investigation of the Neville St Clair affair. Perched on top of his head, perhaps by way of a perverse homage to the Red Headed League was a wig of long, lanky red hair!

'At once, of course, I recognised the full significance of this. You see, that single red strand of hair had saved me from blundering in, and making a fatal error. If I could now separate Morrison from his associates, and catch him unawares, I would have my man. It was obvious that he could ill afford me exposing his true identity to his present company, and any fate he might suffer in police custody would be preferable to the consequences of that.'

By now the speed, and complexity of Holmes's reasoning had left me feeling totally bemused. 'In heaven's name, Holmes, you go too quickly, and assume too much! What may seem obvious to you may not always appear so to lesser mortals,' I protested.

'I humbly apologise, my dear Watson, but the lateness of the hour, and my own natural excitement have let me run away with myself. Yet surely it is now obvious, Constable Parkes was never in any real danger at all.'

'You mean Morrison meant him no harm? Then surely that means Lestrade's theory, regarding Daxer's involvement, was sound all along,' I suggested.

'Watson!' Holmes slapped his forehead with his left palm in exasperation. 'Parkes is Morrison, or, at least he was prior to my subsequent conversation with him.'

'So you are saying that Silas Morrison never really existed at all?' I asked.

'He was merely an invention of Parkes's to help further his investigative career,' Holmes confirmed.

'Of course!' I exclaimed. 'Which is why there were no police records of the night duties that Mrs Mullins was certain he was undertaking. This also explains his incredible success rate. The criminals would bring their ill-gotten goods to Morrison, for him to dispose of, on their behalf, whereupon, in his Parkes persona, he would have them arrested shortly afterwards. It is brilliant, and a compliment to you, and your method.'

'I very much regret that you choose to remind me of the part my own career has played in this sorry affair. My method, and his public trust have both been sadly abused. Do you not remember the list of crime details Lestrade had sent to me?' Holmes asked bitterly. 'More especially the appended list of missing objects.'

'How dull I have been, and what you must now think of me for daring to link his reprehensible behaviour to your method. However, I do remember that in each case there were always items never accounted for. These, I presume, Parkes decided to keep for himself,' I conjectured.

'Ah! At last, I perceive, the first glimmer of realization has dawned on you. Tonight I was in the lair of the archdevil of crime and all his minions. This was a situation which only my own wits could save me from.

'I continued my performance of the drunk, all the while drawing ever closer to Morrison's table. At last I caught his attention. He began abusing me in the vilest, and most raucous of tones and language, and he despatched two of his henchmen to have me removed from his sight.

'The immediate danger was obvious. If I missed my mark now another opportunity might never present itself, so highly did I regard his ability to cover his tracks. In an instant, with the cut-throats just inches from me, I lunged myself towards Morrison, and grabbed at his hair.

' 'I shall wrench this thing from your head in an instant if your next words do not please me, Constable Parkes!' I whispered hoarsely into his ear. Quickly now.

'Everything now rested on my belief that he was clever enough to realize the danger that non-cooperation would place him in.'

' 'Leave 'im to me lads,' he called out breathlessly. 'Me, and my friend are going to take a stroll upstairs and will not take kindly to being disturbed.' In docile obedience his henchmen duly complied, and resumed their seats, grumbling amongst themselves, but obviously under his control.

'Without another word, he led me to a small wooden staircase, concealed behind the bar, which we hastily ascended. Out of the corner of my eye I noticed Shinwell Johnson assume his position at the base of the stairs. As you can imagine, he was a most welcome sight, for if anyone is capable of holding a stairway, it is surely Shinwell Johnson.

'The huge studio room Parkes led me into, I shall no longer refer to him by his pseudonym, contained all the missing pieces to our mystery. While he was securing the door with two large bolts, I looked around and realized that all the personal items on view, were, undoubtedly, those missing from his room at Mrs Mullins's. The large cache of valuables, plate, works of art, and jewellery, were amongst those unaccounted for at the conclusion of his cases.

'Apart from the items I have already mentioned, the room was otherwise quite sparse, so we each took to seating ourselves on two of many tea chests, scattered about the place. To emphasise the harsh reality of his situation I withdrew your army revolver, and kept it to hand while I re-lit my cigarette.

'I admire your courage, Mr Holmes, for coming here tonight without the company of the regular force. Mind you, Lestrade, and his colleagues are probably still expecting to find me within the clutches of foreign conspirators.' Parkes laughed briefly at this before adding: 'I suppose you were confident that your ploy downstairs would have the desired effect on me'. His voice was surprisingly refined, with only the merest trace of a modulated Lancastrian accent.

'Despite the mistakes that you have made, there is a certain cleverness about you that justified my assumption. Besides, I have a stalwart companion below who is more than a match for your new, chosen friends.' I spat out these last words with a certain bitterness.

'Besides which, you had no real proof with which to approach Lestrade, and his friends.' Parkes rejoined. 'It is reassuring to know that even the great Sherlock

Holmes occasionally has to resort to a gamble as his last throw. Incidentally, I have used your method in identifying you. No one else could have been capable of tracing me, and once all other possibilities had been eliminated, I realized that Sherlock Holmes lay beneath that splendid disguise.'

"'I resent the way you have abused my method . . . Mister Parkes! As you know, my work is usually its own reward, while you have sought something far more tangible, and thereby become seduced by it. I presume that you became so involved in your business at this establishment that you realized one of your identities would have to be eliminated. This being the more profitable of the two, the choice, for you, was not a difficult one to make.'

"'More difficult than you might think,' Parkes replied. 'My initial goal was not a financial one, I assure you. I sought to attain your own high level of investigative achievement. Alas, I discovered the former to be the easier to obtain, and certainly the one requiring fewer personal sacrifices. Please also bear in mind, once you, and the police finally bring me to book, that not one soul has suffered injury at my hand, and a large number of odious criminals have been removed from the streets of London as a result of my little masquerade.'

'I was incensed by his off hand manner, and not a little annoyed by his lack of remorse and regret. If he were seeking compliment, or admonishment from me, despite the numerous compliments he had already paid me, he was to be sadly disappointed. I decided to terminate this unsavoury interview at once.

''I feel we shall both be safer if we retain our disguises until we reach the sanctuary of Scotland Yard. Perhaps the more so for you than for me.' Was my only response. I had observed a small panel cut into the wall at the rear of the room. This, I had correctly surmised opened to a secret exit that led to a narrow alley that ran down the side of the building. Consequently, we made safely away, the presence of your revolver rendering Parkes harmless.

'My only regret was being unable to get

word of our escape to Johnson till hours later. However, he has emerged from the adventure unscathed, and Parkes now languishes behind bars, where, I trust our system of justice will ensure he remains for some considerable time.'

'My dear Holmes! What a truly remarkable story,' I exclaimed, taken aback and quite breathless with excitement.

'Ah, but we are not quite finished yet, Watson. It is now imperative that we snatch a few hours of sorely needed sleep, so that we are fully prepared for the morning.'

'I cannot argue with that,' I said rising from my chair. 'Yet I fail to see what yet remains to be done. You have performed the task so thoroughly.'

'I mentioned before that I rarely seek any kind of reward for my work. On this occasion I am prepared to make an exception. I must be fit enough to enjoy the look on Lestrade's face when he finds Parkes residing in his cell later this morning!'

The Adventure of the Dying Gaul

The inexplicably early retirement of my old friend and colleague, Sherlock Holmes, to the tranquillity of the Sussex coast in the year 1903, has, obviously, left a huge vacuum in my life. That is not to say the occasional puzzle has not attracted Holmes's attention and from time to time he has even requested my assistance in the solving of these. However, these episodes have been few and far between and only a handful of these cases have been worthy of note.

Consequently I have come to rely on my own small practice as a means of filling my days, my evenings occupied in a constant reappraisal of my old case notes, within the confines of my new rooms in Queen Anne Street. Initially it came as some surprise to me to discover the absence of any notes relating to the first half of the year 1898. This dearth of information was harder to explain when I recalled the great demand Holmes's services had been put under during much of that period. However, much of his work was undertaken alone while I spent weeks agonising and speculating at our rooms in Baker Street, not seeing or hearing from Holmes for a fortnight or more.

This pattern of behaviour was not uncommon in my friend, yet the increasing length of time that passed between each of our meetings surely was. When this silence was finally broken, however, Holmes's choice of words brought back to life the most calamitous period of our association.

'I propose that you come away with me for a week onto the continent,' Holmes said suddenly one morning over breakfast. Strangely, the significance of this invitation struck not the slightest chord in the memory of my friend, although it had been with these very words that he had initiated our flight from the odious Professor Moriarty, an exodus culminating in their tumultuous struggle at the

Reichenbach falls in 1891. My reaction to these words was lost on Holmes, who rapidly continued. 'To the city of Rome, to be more precise, if it is not inconvenient to you.'

By now my attention had been drawn to a note that had evidently been delivered prior to my coming down to breakfast, and the sight of this immediately dispelled the ghosts of seven years' past.

'To Rome?!' I exclaimed. 'By all means, dear fellow, but what event could possibly necessitate such a journey?'

Seated opposite me, at our dining table, and enjoying his third cigarette since the conclusion of our meal, Holmes could barely conceal his pleasure at receiving this summons and he held the note tantalisingly before him.

'Ha, Watson! I take it you have heard of that venerable institution, ensconced within the eternal city, known as the Capitoline museum. Equally, I am sure you know of the valuable and extensive collection of antique statues that it houses.'

'Why yes, of course!' I replied firmly.

'Excellent, then I am sure you are aware that the collection's renowned centrepiece is the majestic statute of 'The Dying Gaul'.'

'Again, yes.' I replied, slowly wearying of Holmes's prevarication.

'Well then, perhaps I can at least surprise you by stating categorically that, as of yesterday morning, 'The Dying Gaul' resides there no more!' Holmes concluded, with a dramatic flourish of the note he still held.

'It has been removed?' I asked speculatively.

'No, friend Watson, it has been stolen!' Holmes exclaimed.

'Good heavens! Then that message is surely from the Rome police force requesting your assistance,' I conjectured.

'Excellent Watson, though they of course prefer the word 'Polizia' however, are you willing to join me on such a mission?'

'By all means! My own work at the surgery has not been too pressing of late and the city of Rome does hold certain attractions. But how was the deed done? I understand the statue is quite a substantial one.'

Flicking the message with some disdain, Holmes emitted a strange growl.

'No details at all! Not one fact worthy of note. We are promised all relevant information upon reaching the terminus of Rome, where we shall be met by their chief of police, Signor Gialli. However, in true Italian style, whatever the message lacks in hard facts is more than made up for by its poetic content. For example, they use this elegant piece of prose as a means to entice me to take up their case. Holmes now read from the note:

'*IT IS ESSENTIAL THAT YOU COME AT ONCE, FOR THIS MAGNIFICENT STATUE IS THE CENTRAL CROWN OF OUR COLLECTION. THE SIMPLE, NATURAL FLOW OF THE POSITION OF THE BODY, THE FACE THAT EXPRESSES PROFOUND ANGUISH WHILE YET EXCUDING GREAT DIGNITY IN THE MIDST OF SUFFERING, ALL COMBINE TO REALIZE THIS WORK AS ONE OF THE MOST OUTSTANDING EXAMPLES OF A SCULPTURE FROM THE ANCIENT WORLD* . . . and so it continues. You shall be glad to know that I have already sent a reply, to the effect that we should be honoured to accept the challenge of their commission,' Holmes concluded.

'I am surprised that you accepted on my behalf prior to consulting me,' I replied in mock indignation.

'If I do not know my Watson after these many years in harness, I would surely be a very poor detective. Besides, the many hours you have spent over your morning papers, of late, have told me of a most slack surgery indeed!'

'Even so, Holmes,' I continued to remonstrate. 'A journey to Rome is not to be taken so lightly.'

'Quite so,' Holmes agreed. 'However, I do wish you would make up your mind without further delay. We must depart in ten minutes, if we are to catch our boat-train!' With that Holmes strode to his room, leaving me aghast at the table, mid way through draining my last cup of tea.

My military training meant that I was well able to meet our departure time and with minutes to spare. However, as our hansom made its way through the hectic thoroughfares of London towards the station, I was forced to reflect on how bizarre my situation truly was; I had just removed myself from a warm comfortable room, a cheery fire, even my cup of tea, and was now hurtling towards the capital city of the ancient world, in order to recover an antique statue at the request of the Rome police.

Undoubtedly my association with Sherlock Holmes had provided me with much to be grateful for, the unique opportunities for adventure, the privilege of observing the remarkable powers of the world's finest detective at first hand, and of course, literary accolades, to mention but three. However, I was equally certain that Holmes would be hard put to find another companion who was as willing to self-sacrifice, on his behalf, as I had been.

As if conscious of my innermost thoughts, Holmes suddenly turned towards me.

'You know, Watson, it really is too good of you to accompany me on this little jaunt. I must say, however, that it promises to provide us with our greatest challenge and adventure to date.'

With that Holmes lapsed into one of

his introspective silences and I was left to reflect that the thrill of adventure that I was experiencing was well worth everything I had left behind me in Baker Street.

We arrived at Charing Cross with barely five minutes to spare before our train's ten o'clock departure. However, we were able to find our first-class carriage with ease and we enjoyed a relaxed, express journey to Folkestone. Somewhat surprisingly, as our journey progressed, I became aware of my friend's increasingly pensive mood.

By the time we had reached Folkestone, I was no nearer to discovering the cause of Holmes's change of demeanour and soon after gave up the thankless task of attempting to guess this. During the course of our smooth crossing to Boulogne, the bracing sea air found me up on deck enjoying its revitalising effects. All the while, Holmes kept himself to the lounge below, smoking his way through an apparently inexhaustible supply of cigarettes.

Our next connection, a train from Boulogne to Paris, afforded us little time to collect ourselves. Indeed, our schedule was so tight that the platform gates were on the point of closing when we arrived at the Paris platform. So it was not until the longest stretch of our journey, from Paris to Turin, was under way that we were allowed some time to relax. A light meal in the above average dining-car was more than a little welcome, yet it was only once our pipes had been lit that I became aware of Holmes's decision to confide in me finally.

He glanced furtively at me a couple of times between long, deep draws on his cherrywood, and then he leant forward, with his elbows balanced on his bony knees.

'I am loath to admit,' he slowly began, 'that I have done you a grave injustice, Watson. Indeed, my very motive, for asking you to accompany me to Rome, was partly based on a deception.'

'What can you possibly mean?!' I asked incredulously. 'Are you saying 'The Dying Gaul' has not been stolen at all?'

Holmes shook his head vehemently several times. 'No, no, no . . . of course not, but I am certain that if I had made my true intention clear to you from the outset you would never have agreed to have come.'

My reply did not disguise the hurt that his remark had caused me. 'I cannot believe that you have dismissed my loyalty so lightly. Throughout the most outlandish mysteries and the gravest of dangers, I have always been your man!'

'Watson, your loyalty and bravery are beyond question,' Holmes responded with earnest. 'And yet if I had divulged the fact that I have deduced the genius and guiding hand of Professor Moriarty behind the theft, even you would surely have denounced me as a madman and abandoned me to my own devices! Now, you cannot deny that this is true.'

I was so shaken and taken aback at the mere mention of that dreadful name that I confess I could not readily deny Holmes's assertions. The name Moriarty was, to me, synonymous with feelings of great sadness and loss and one I had never expected to hear again, save in a fleeting reference to the past. To hear

Holmes now mention that name again, in reference to a contemporary crime, seemed anomalous at the very least!

I am ashamed to admit that my initial diagnosis was that a reversion to his long dormant habit of taking cocaine had resulted in what was, surely, a sad delusion. Yet, as I stared at his keen, alert face from across our carriage and observed the bright intensity of his eyes, I confess there was no medical evidence of that awful habit having returned. I decided that the answer must lie elsewhere.

'It would seem, therefore, that my deception was necessary,' Holmes gravely pronounced, somehow sensing my scepticism. 'Necessary, but not justified. You certainly deserve better than this at my hand. You must understand, however, that this bizarre deduction of mine, has not been conceived merely from the events at the Capitoline. It is the culmination of a line of thought that first emerged four years ago. Dormant, sometimes for months on end, then suddenly regenerated by an event, on the Continent, or a certain inquiry bearing new fruit.'

As Holmes continued speaking, my initial horror and disbelief were slowly dispelled. I remembered that I was seated opposite the world's most logical and dispassionate mind, as devoid of delusion and fancy as it is possible to conceive. As exasperating as this trait of his could be at times, it nonetheless, reminded me now that his theory, concerning Moriarty, was undoubtedly well founded and a sudden thrill swept through me.

Holmes seemed to recognise this marked change in my attitude towards him and his theory, and he elaborated with increased excitement.

'It was your own heartfelt, though erroneous, chronicling of my conflict with Moriarty in the story you entitled, the 'Final Problem', that initiated my long line of thought. The specific focus of interest being your reference to his brother, the Colonel, whose existence had up to that point been unknown to me.

'As you are aware, Watson, my investigation into Moriarty's life and organisation, throughout the months leading up to our final confrontation, had been most detailed and thorough. Yet my inquiries were restricted to his criminal activities alone, and perhaps I would have been better served if I had expanded my field of vision to encompass his family also. For at no stage was I aware of the existence of the Colonel. Yet no sooner was Moriarty pronounced dead and discredited than the Colonel suddenly appeared in his defence, and at the expense of my own good name. Then, only to disappear again just as mysteriously. I was forced, therefore, to question to what extent the Colonel had been involved in his late brother's activities.

'At this point certain contradictions in the professor's character and behaviour began manifesting themselves to me. Though twisted and perverse in the extreme, it is worth remembering that the professor's mind was as logical and analytical as my own. The 'intellectual treat' he had enjoyed in observing my efforts in bringing him down, was shared by me in observing the subtlety and intricacy of his operations, though of course, I was loath to admit it at the time.

'Such a mind would surely have devised a more subtle defence, against my final thrust, than merely chasing us in a train. I now feel certain that he would have been aware of the futility of such action, bearing in mind that the final closing of the trap was going to take place with or without my presence in London. Such time as he wasted in his pursuit of us would, surely, have been better spent in devising a means of thwarting me, even at the last. You see, Watson, I began deducing contradiction after contradiction. He did not even await the outcome of my *coup de grâce* on the Monday, preferring to pursue us blindly to the Continent, giving no consideration to his fate should he have decided to return to London at the conclusion of his journey.

'However, the most deviant aspect of his behaviour, throughout, was the manner of his attack upon me at the Reichenbach Falls, although you will appreciate that the urgency of the situation precluded any such reflective thought at the time! I am sure you can recall my description of the man and, therefore, that he was not someone readily disposed to acts of violent physical action. Indeed, years of scholastic study had evolved him into a purely mental entity, his body, merely a means of conveying his thoughts and perverse ideas for his minions then to act upon. No, Watson, the very idea of such an attack would have been totally abhorrent to him, and unnecessary, when you consider that he was accompanied by the equally odious but decidedly more lethal Colonel Sebastian Moran.

'The years have not dulled my memory of that fateful moment. As I stood with my back to the falls, I was certain that I was at the mercy of Professor Moriarty, yet now, in retrospect, I can see much room for doubt. Consider Watson, the air was thick with the mists from the thundering falls, Moriarty's collar and muffler were worn high and his hat rim brought down low. His obscured features were contorted by violent rage. Furthermore he displayed a strength that I would not, previously, have credited him with.

Truly, if I were to stand in a court room today, I could not swear on oath that it was the professor whom I sent hurtling to his death within the depths of that terrible chasm.'

Holmes paused for a moment, to refill and relight his pipe.

'I must truly congratulate you, Holmes!' I stated in breathless excitement. 'This is surely the finest achievement in deductive reasoning that you have attained to date.'

'Ah, so Watson, the cynic, has now become enlightened. You have, no doubt, now perceived that this is no wild theory of mine, but a gradual dissection of a great falsehood, that may yet cost me dear.'

'How so?' I asked.

'To make this clear to you I will now have to impart more recent evidence and add this to my hypothesis of the past. My previous investigations on the Continent have realized me many contacts within each country's respective police force. They have been more than obliging in providing me with information pertaining to all noteworthy crimes that have occurred within their jurisdiction over the past four years.'

'Why just those specific years?' I asked.

'Because they are the only years that are relevant. Assuming the accuracy of my theory, the professor, upon learning of his brother's death at the falls, would immediately have gone into hiding perhaps in a recess or labyrinth, prepared some years before, for such an unfortunate eventuality. No doubt Colonel Moran and, perhaps, a minion or two, who had escaped my net, would serve to protect the professor's secret and provide him with news of the outside world.

'Our ruse and entrapment of Colonel Moran that night at the 'Empty House' deprived the professor of his last significant ally, and would surely have spurred his flight to the Continent. My calculation of four years is based on the assumption that it would take him a year, at the least, to assume a new identity and re-build his organisation.

'I must conclude that my calculation has been an accurate one. Every police force, that I have maintained contact with, has reported an increase in organised crime during this period. His hallmarks are clear enough to see. Each crime has been organised down to the smallest detail and is distinguished by its intricate, long-term planning. Naturally, on those rare occasions when the crime has been thwarted, the threads never lead to the central core. Watson, professor Moriarty is now the principal moving force behind the worst of continental crime and, it seems that his voracious talons have now extended to Rome.

'Incidentally, Watson, two most damning and suggestive pieces of evidence have come to my attention only recently. The birth records of both brothers were mysteriously destroyed by fire some years ago whilst the existence of a third, younger brother has also come to light. Whilst I do not suggest that he was in any way connected with the criminal activities of his elder brothers, being a popular station-master in the West Country, it is somewhat suggestive to note that he was killed in a train accident, exactly four years ago!'

I sank back in my seat, mentally exhausted by the extent of Holmes's faculty for deduction and the sensational nature of its conclusion.

'Well, Moriarty certainly covers his tracks with ruthless efficiency,' I observed.

Holmes nodded solemnly. 'Indeed he does and I have allowed him to entrench himself in his new criminal habitat as deeply as he once was in London. For the past four years I have been a worthless fool, pursuing my own career. All the while, the man whom I thought I had destroyed has rendered my other successes meaningless. By the way, Watson, be in no doubt as to the danger of our position once we begin our work in Rome. I am sure that Moriarty will recognise my hand as surely as I have his.'

'Are the Rome police aware of the situation?' I asked.

'They are most anxious to help, in their own inept way, yet, so far, have discovered nothing to indicate the involvement of Moriarty. Ah, but now I fancy, we begin the approach to the station of Turin. A chance time lapse between our trains will allow us the opportunity for some refreshment, I think.'

I was glad of the break in our travels, for my head was spinning with the speed of our progress and the length and drama of Holmes's narrative. As I was to discover, on our return journey, we had passed through hundreds of miles of the most breathtaking and scenic landscapes that Europe has to offer. Yet I had been so spellbound at each of Holmes's words that I had missed it all. Though generally speaking more appreciative of my natural surroundings than Holmes ever was, I was not a bit surprised that I had been oblivious to them on this occasion, nor was I resentful at having been so.

Thankfully we were both able to sleep during our journey's final leg, and we arrived at the terminus in Rome in time for an early breakfast, barely twenty four hours after we had deserted our rooms in Baker Street.

We were met on the platform by two very smart uniformed officers who, after collecting our luggage from the luggage-van, led us to a gracious Landau that awaited us outside. Here we were greeted by our host and colleague, Inspector Gialli.

Clearly the officers spoke not a word of English, but Inspector Gialli, to our pleasant surprise, had a reasonable command of our language and offered to act as both our interpreter and collaborator throughout the duration of our stay. For ease of narrative, I shall eliminate his many errors in interpretation and pronunciation.

'Good morning, gentlemen!' He smiled, as he stepped down lightly from the carriage. 'I trust your journey was pleasant?'

'Indeed it was, Inspector. It was good of you to meet us at such an hour,' I replied, bowing politely. Holmes seemed to be amused by the appearance of our host and barely suppressed a smile as he bowed in turn.

Gialli was quite short for a policeman, standing at little more than five feet six inches. His build and posture can best be described as neat and dapper; from his light grey bowler down to his gaiters he exuded a certain elegance. His facial expressions were charming. He sported a tiny though well waxed moustache. Yet the items that distinguished him the most from his London counterparts, were his exuberantly patterned tie and a pale grey top-coat that he wore unbuttoned.

His light-hearted manner certainly belied his profession, and his attitude and conversation, the awesome task before us. He chatted incessantly about his desire to visit London and then, apologetically, about the unseasonably cold weather, that Rome was experiencing at that time. For myself, having so recently left the chill of London, I found it uncomfortably warm in my heavy coat.

Holmes held a stony silence throughout our journey to the hotel which the Roman authorities had provided for us. I, on the other hand, found my attention being constantly diverted, from our host's conversation, by the wondrous edifices, both ancient and renaissance, that consistently lined our route.

Gialli noted my fascination with these

surroundings and proceeded to identify many of the places of interest which we passed, with an understandable pride. I soon lost track of the numerous churches, forums, temples and piazzas that Gialli was describing. Indeed I was looking forward to a few hours rest at our hotel, when we pulled up outside another magnificent building, on the Via Nationale, which, in any other city in the world, would surely have been described as a palace. I was astounded to learn that this imposing monument was to serve as our accommodation for the next few days! Holmes, however, with his usual cold, diffident air might have just pulled up outside 221b Baker Street, for all the effect his surroundings had on him.

'I should like to visit the museum at ten o'clock,' he informed Gialli, to my great horror, for this rendezvous would only afford us two hours' rest.

'Surely a visit in the early afternoon would suit just as well? I am completely spent!' I protested.

Holmes turned on me with a glare. 'Watson! The scent is cold enough as it is and Moriarty is not one to delay in obscuring his tracks.' With that he bounded up the hotel stairs and left me exhausted at the bottom.

To Holmes's intense annoyance, it was not until a quarter past the agreed hour that we received the message that Inspector Gialli awaited our pleasure in the lobby below.

A short journey in the landau took us past the ancient market and forum of the Emperor Trajan and around the base of the half completed monument to King Victor Emmanuel, before delivering us to the foot of the magnificent staircase that stretches up to the Capitol. It was only upon discovering that the building at the top of the steps was, indeed, the Capitoline museum, that Holmes finally became attentive to his surroundings.

Almost at once his features took on an entirely different aspect. His eyes seemed to spring to life, darting from side to side, alert to any potential clue, while his face became taut and hungry. Ignoring the unique equestrian statue of Marcus Aurelius, that stood guard before the museum, Holmes made for the entrance with a decided spring in his step.

At once, he began making enquiries as to the security arrangements on the day of the theft. Holmes asked me to make appropriate notes, as a plethora of information began cascading upon us from Gialli, his subordinates, and the head of the museum's security guards. However, Holmes soon realized that the only fact, worthy of attention, was that two of the guards, on duty that day, were only engaged some three weeks prior to the theft.

'You can see here, Watson, how vital is my ability to sift the relevant information from the superfluous. The task of examining every detail and gorging oneself on a stew of useless information is both time consuming and dulling to the senses. However, even at this stage of our investigation, I can perceive the direction our inquiries must immediately take.'

To emphasise his point, Holmes at once requested that Gialli despatch two of his officers to locate the source of employment of the two guards in question. We were denied the opportunity of interviewing these two, by reason of their unexplained absence from work for the past two days, though, in truth, Holmes seemed hardly surprised to learn of this.

With Gialli and myself in his wake, Holmes strode purposefully through the front hall, oblivious to the miraculous examples of ancient sculpture, by which he was surrounded, and called back to request directions to the famous First Room, from where 'The Dying Gaul' had been removed. Upon being informed that it was located on the upper floor, Holmes bounded up the stairs ahead of us, and was already examining a large empty plinth, in the centre of the room, with his glass, by the time Gialli and I joined him. I motioned to Gialli to remain silent and still whilst Holmes continued his work. A moment later Holmes straightened himself and, with an impatient grunt, snapped his glass away. He glared accusingly at Inspector Gialli.

'Inspector,' Holmes began, with some annoyance. 'Someone has very carefully removed all of the traces that might have proved useful to me!'

'Signor Holmes, I can assure you that none of the officers under my control, would have been so stupid as to remove anything at all from the scene of a crime!' Gialli replied, his round face alight with indignation. 'However, I understand from yourself that the man you suspect of being the mastermind behind the theft, is of above average intellect. Therein, I suspect, lies your explanation.'

'I can assure you that I meant no disrespect,' Holmes mumbled apologetically. 'Perhaps my experience of the London police force has made me, somewhat cynical. Now, you must describe to me, in exact and concise terms, the full circumstances of the theft of 'The Dying Gaul'.' As he spoke, Holmes seated himself on the empty plinth, in readiness.

Aghast at Holmes's apparent irreverence, Gialli eyed him quizzically, for a moment, before proceeding.

'The alarm was first raised by the very two guards who have, subsequently, gone missing. They were on duty that morning in the Fifth Room, otherwise known as the Bust Room. This room contains an unequalled collection of Imperial portraits, that are both entirely authentic and, of course, irreplaceable.

'It seems that a member of the viewing public was suddenly taken by a violent attack of brain fever and was endeavouring to vandalise the magnificent head of Caracalla with a pocket knife. No doubt due to their relative lack of experience, in such a situation, our guards called for immediate assistance, whereupon the manager and several other guards raced to their aid.

'By the time this entourage had entered the Bust Room, they discovered that the malefactor had disappeared, but that only slight damage had been inflicted on the bust. A thorough search was conducted of all the adjacent galleries, but to no avail. After being questioned by the police, the guards, who had raised the alarm, were allowed to leave and have not been seen since.'

Gialli paused for a moment and stared, intently, into the eyes of Sherlock

Holmes, before continuing.

'Ah, but now to the most perplexing aspect of our little mystery,' Gialli smiled mischievously, obviously fully aware of my friend's penchant for the more unusual aspects of crime.

Holmes's head jerked up, suddenly, with a look of hungry anticipation upon his face, very like an epicure waiting to be served with a gourmet meal.

With increased excitement, Gialli continued:

'Despite the furore created by the incident in the Bust Room, and despite the easy access and wide berth afforded by the main entrance, no attempt was made at removing 'The Dying Gaul' through that route!'

'You are sure of this?' Holmes asked, up on his feet once more, while trying to gauge the distance between the vacant plinth and the front entrance.

'There is no doubt of it, Signor. Two guards at the entrance were put on their vigil at the first sign of trouble and secured the main entrance until my men arrived shortly afterwards. They have both affirmed that no attempt was made to pass them by persons either with, or without, the missing statue,' Gialli earnestly replied.

'Yet I am sure, a building such as this, has more than one exit, does it not?' Holmes asked confidently. By now he had ceased his pacing. He placed his foot upon the plinth and rested his left elbow upon his knee, while he tried to visualise the chain of events that Gialli had just outlined.

'Assuredly,' Gialli replied. 'Yet it is located at the far side of the building, and can only be reached by passing through a number of the other galleries. However that was, without doubt, the route taken by the thieves. The solid oak door was broken down and used as a means to traverse a stretch of mud that part of the original path has degenerated into. I do not understand it, Signor Holmes. For two determined men the front exit would be a far easier option, as I will now demonstrate.'

Gialli then proceeded to lead us on a trek through a veritable labyrinth of rooms and galleries, each containing striking images of the ancient past. With each room that we passed through on our ten minute journey, I became increasingly convinced that the thieves had undertaken a most foolhardy and perilous task. The more so when I considered the heavy weight of the object that they were attempting to procure. Holmes seemed similarly perplexed, no doubt wondering at the fact that the mind of Professor Moriarty was, supposedly, behind the planning of this scheme.

Upon reaching the far-flung escape route, we found that things were exactly as they had been described to us by our Roman colleague. We could see that the large wooden door had been used as a flat bridge to ease the transport of so cumbersome an object, from the doorway to the dry path beyond.

Holmes immediately withdrew his glass and used it to scour the door and the gravel path for footprints and clues. He raised himself from the ground a few moments later and I was disappointed to note that there was not even a hint of success on his face. Gialli, evidently shared my disappointment, for he began tutting to himself and bemoaned the fate of the statue under his breath.

Then, as Holmes began re-crossing the 'bridge' he suddenly stopped in his tracks. 'What is this?' he cried, while dropping to the ground once more. 'Ha!' was followed by 'Excellent!' and then, while still holding his glass, he summoned us both to join him. Offering his glass to each of us in turn, he indicated a small, almost invisible, scratch etched into the outer rim of the door.

Much to Holmes's obvious impatience, Gialli and I exchanged glances that indicated our mutual confusion.

'Do you not see?!' Holmes exclaimed. He then continued in the most urgent manner. 'It is small certainly, indeed I almost passed over it myself, and, initially appears to be most insignificant. Yet it is most certainly an indication that the foot of one of our intruders, missed its mark and slipped from the edge of the door. Upon realizing this, I merely cast my gaze two inches to the left and discovered this . . . ' He diverted our attention towards a lightly indented, yet clearly defined boot mark in the surrounding mud.

Holmes jumped up immediately and ushered us back into the building. 'Now, Inspector, there is a certain theory that I wish to put to the test. To do so I shall require the co-operation of you and two of your most stalwart officers. I should be pleased if they could meet me at this door, conveying a statue of similar size and weight to 'The Dying Gaul' in as short a time as possible.' With that Holmes turned away to re-examine the path.

'What theory can he possibly mean?' Gialli asked of me in exasperation.

'I cannot even speculate myself,' I replied. 'Yet he certainly has one, so my advice to you would be to set his arrangements in motion with all speed. You will find that it is in your best interests to do so.'

Gialli threw his arms up in the air and violently shook his head in a true Latin pique, before departing on his errand.

Upon his return Gialli was accompanied by two enormous policemen who, at well over six feet in height, were both tall and broad. 'I think that they enjoy the pasta a little too much!' was Gialli's attempt at a mood lightening jest. This was shared and enjoyed, after translation, by his colleagues, but not by Holmes who was solemnly shaking his head upon his return from his search of the path.

'The large gravel content of the path renders the task of assimilating clues an impossible one. Ah, but Inspector you have done exceedingly well!' Holmes exclaimed, upon noticing a large statue of Perseus resting on the floor behind the hefty policemen.

'Now, gentlemen, if one of you would be so kind as to stand over here in the mud, remaining there, quite still for a moment or two,' Holmes requested, by way of a translation from Gialli. Once Holmes's request was made known to them, the two officers could barely suppress their amusement at the strange ways of the English detective. This display of mirth, I was pleased to note, was immediately reprimanded with an icy stare from their superior.

The policemen immediately carried out Holmes's bidding and then stood back whilst Holmes threw himself down to the ground once more to examine the newly created boot prints. Apparently satisfied with his discovery, Holmes then asked both officers to lift up the statue and carry it to a patch of flat, even mud close by the newly made prints. They wielded this edifice with surprising and casual ease and carried it over to the precise spot, standing motionless with it, until such time as Holmes was satisfied. Thereupon, through the translation of Gialli once more, Holmes thanked the two men for their co-operation and asked them to return Perseus to his original berth.

Still bearing the expression of confusion, the two men returned to the museum whilst Holmes bent over the fresh prints, and busied himself for a few moments with his glass and a measuring tape that he always carried with him. Upon rising once more, Holmes looked pensively from Gialli to myself and then to Gialli again finally realizing, from our expressions, that an explanation was now necessary.

'Oh, but surely gentlemen, is the thing not obvious?' Holmes asked, with a light laugh. Despite his condescending tone, Gialli and I listened intently to his every word. 'Inspector, your very own testimony has eliminated the possibility that the statue was removed through the building's main entrance. Whilst my own simple experiment will prove conclusively that 'The Dying Gaul' did not pass this way either. You see, the depth of the boot print, created by our clumsy intruder was matched precisely by that of the officer who stood in the mud, empty-handed. However the depths of the prints, created once your men were incommoded by the statue, were considerably greater. Therefore, because we have proven that the statue can be nowhere else, I have concluded that 'The Dying Gaul' still resides within the confines of the museum!'

'Holmes, why should anyone go to such

lengths and take such risks only to leave the object that they have sought behind them when they leave?' I asked him sceptically. Then, to my surprise, Gialli pre-empted Holmes's reply.

'Ah, Signor Holmes, I think that I understand you now! During the past three weeks the intruders, masquerading as the missing security guards, have been discreetly preparing a hiding place, wherein to secrete the statue while all attention was being diverted to the incident in the Bust Room. This will allow them to return for the statue at a time when the risk has been greatly minimised. Naturally, they will have assumed that their ruse will have successfully caused us to broaden our search beyond the confines of the museum.'

Holmes clapped his hands excitedly: 'Excellent Inspector! Your insight into the incident is almost as clear as my own. Of course, their plan might well have succeeded, had I not observed that minuscule mark on the fallen door, and even now we and your men would be conducting a fruitless search for a statue that was under our noses all the time!'

'There is a mind of great guile and cunning behind this scheme,' Gialli gravely pronounced.

I glanced at Holmes and saw that he had paled visibly at this suggestion, as if a large, dark cloud had passed overhead.

'Moriarty?' I suggested, in a tone of quiet reverence that the name hardly deserved.

'Ah, of course, this demonic professor of yours, Signor Holmes,' Gialli rejoined. 'Alas, however, our inquiries so far have revealed no evidence of his presence here in Rome.'

'Yet he is here, I am sure of it,' said Holmes, his voice almost inaudible.

'However, we have no reasonable means of closing in on him until such time as those two elusive guards have been located and prevailed upon to assist us. In the meantime, I suggest that we return to our most luxurious hotel and obtain some sorely needed sustenance and rest.'

'But what of 'The Dying Gaul'?' Gialli

exclaimed, aghast.

'I have no means of knowing its exact location within the building,' Holmes admitted casually. 'So, short of pulling up every marble slab in the museum, I suggest, Inspector, that you mount a most vigilant, yet discreet, twenty-four hour guard. Rest assured, the gang will return soon enough and unwittingly do the hard work for us. Come Watson!'

Gialli shot me a parting glance of despair, but I had no answer for him and was merely carried along by Holmes's irresistible wash. I was partly surprised and resentful at leaving the scene of the crime when a satisfactory conclusion was so nearly in our grasp. Yet I was equally glad that Holmes shared my need for food and rest, and I was determined to seize this opportunity.

This I surely did, and apart from a brief awakening in the early evening during which time I took a light supper in my room, I slept straight through till eleven o'clock the following morning. Despite the stimulation, provided by the events of the previous day, mine had been a deep, dreamless sleep and I awoke fully refreshed and more than a little ready for my breakfast.

With this in mind, I hastened to my friend's room only to find, upon enquiring in the lobby, that he had gone out earlier after taking directions to the Roman Forum. It seemed that the allure of ancient Rome was too strong even for Sherlock Holmes to resist. I breakfasted alone, therefore, and it was not until mid-afternoon that Holmes finally returned from his excursion. He appeared to be surprisingly drawn and exhausted. In contrast to my own rejuvenated demeanour and in answer to my look of concern and sympathy he replied:

'This interminable waiting is considerably more taxing than any form of vigorous activity. If I see one more broken column, or ancient stone I shall surely despair! I take it no word has come as yet from Gialli. Tut, tut, I thought as much. I think that I shall smoke in my room for a while. Perhaps Gialli will make some progress this afternoon.' Before I had the chance to utter even a single word of response, Holmes was gone!

As it transpired, Holmes's estimate of the time required for Gialli's inquiries to yield success proved to be optimistic in the extreme. An afternoon turned into a day and then two and all the while Holmes became more agitated and his excursions, from the hotel, more seldom. He remained in his room for the most part, smoking incessantly and only occasionally did he take advantage of the excellent cuisine provided by our hotel's dining-room.

During the long agonising wait, I spent much of my time in marvelling at the splendour of St Peter's or lost in wonder at the awesome Colosseum. Yet always, upon my return to the hotel, I was confronted by the sight of my poor friend's continued frustration and progressive dissipation. My concern for Holmes was on the point of becoming despair, when we were awoken at dawn the following morning, with news from Gialli at the museum.

Gialli had not come to the hotel to meet us, preferring, most commendably, to remain on site and organise the initial inquiries. However, the messenger he had despatched with our carriage carried a brief note which informed us of an attempted breach of security at the museum in the early hours of the morning. When I conveyed this information to Holmes who was, inevitably, smoking in his room, the change that came over him was as startling as it was immediate. By the time that he had joined me in the waiting landau outside, the transformation was complete. He even proffered me a jovial slap on the shoulders as he sprang into the carriage.

The driver was obviously under instructions from Gialli, for he moved off and made directly for the Capitoline without any prompting from us.

'Watson,' Holmes began excitedly. 'Perhaps the game is not yet lost! If my surmise is correct and Gialli has followed my instructions exactly, I am sure we shall discover our elusive guards under close arrest upon our arrival at the museum.'

Sure enough, when Gialli greeted us at

the base of the Capitoline steps there was a faint red tint of pleasure and excitement upon his round cheeks. He was, without doubt, in awe of his English confederate and greeted Holmes with a pronounced bow. Characteristically, Holmes dismissed this with a casual wave of the hand, immediately demanding information as he sprang down from the carriage.

Gialli shook Holmes warmly by the hand: 'I congratulate you, Signor Holmes. The initial testimony of our two prisoners has confirmed each one of your deductions. Every honour that is in the power of the city of Rome to bestow, now awaits you!' Then, observing how unimpressed Holmes was by this proclamation, Gialli hurriedly continued. 'Unfortunately there is still no news, nor information that can shed any light on the whereabouts of your professor, however the facts are these.' While Gialli was speaking we had begun the long climb up the steps to the Capitol.

'Acting upon your most excellent advice, I have left in place a rigid, though discreet, guard of my finest men at the museum, every night since your examination. This morning, at exactly four o'clock, my men were alerted to the sounds of a forced entry. Upon my instruction, they took great care not to confront the intruders, instead taking to pre-arranged places of concealment, in order to observe developments.

'These quickly followed. The intruders, swiftly and silently removed the plinth vacated by 'The Dying Gaul' and then prised out the marble slab that had supported it. This revealed a shallow, but precisely cut hollow in which the missing statue has lain unharmed all this time!

'My men were on the intruders in an instant. Being outnumbered by a ratio of three to one, the intruders soon recognised the hopelessness of their situation, gave up the struggle and succumbed to their arrest.

'By the time I had responded to my summons and arrived at the museum, the thieves had sunk into a most melancholy mood, no doubt induced by their dread of impending imprisonment. However various promises I made to them of assistance at their trial, should they cooperate, soon helped me extricate the missing details from their cowardly tongues,' Gialli triumphantly concluded.

'Inspector Gialli, you and your men have performed most admirably from first to last! However, if I might crave your indulgence for just a moment or two, I think that I might be able to pre-empt those missing details?' Holmes requested.

Gialli gladly nodded his assent.

'After all,' Holmes began, 'the majority of the facts are already in our possession. The visitor with the brain-fever was, undoubtedly, a confederate of the masquerading guards and it was he, with one other, who concealed the statue beneath the plinth while the other personnel were being lured to the Bust Room and beyond. During the ensuing confusion they would have all fled the building through the side exit, in the manner we discovered the other day. Obviously they expected us to believe that 'The Dying Gaul' went with them.'

'A most ingenious plan and one which surely would have succeeded, but for your astute foresight and intervention, Signor Holmes,' Gialli enthusiastically rejoined. 'The City of Rome owes you a huge debt, Signor Holmes.'

'Gratifying though your relief at the statue's recovery surely is, the more so, for the apprehension of the culprits, my own overriding interest really resides with the location and destruction of their far more important and dangerous employer. Therefore, I should be glad if you would perform for me one last service as interpreter,' Holmes asked of Gialli as we entered the Capitoline.

Upon entering the First Room once more, we could see 'The Dying Gaul' being returned to its original resting-place and immediately I could see why its supposed theft had led to such furore. I am sure that there can be no finer example of the sculptor's art in existence and I was immediately struck by the effect of animation the artist had imbued into his stone. The subject was undoubtedly a fallen barbarian warrior and yet the sculptor had surely been sympathetic towards his subject, for, though the face conveyed much pain and suffering, there was a certain noble defiance depicted also.

The raucous wailing of the two prisoners huddled on the floor in a corner surrounded by policemen, jolted me from my contemplation and Gialli led us over to them so that Holmes could begin his interviews.

The two rogues were most singular, by virtue of their contrasting appearance. The one responsible for that awful wailing certainly belied his striking visual impact, being tall, muscular and blond. Indeed his stone effigy would not have been out of place within our present surroundings. His partner, however, was dark of skin, swarthy of complexion and he sat in a morose silence, sporting at the least, two days' facial hair.

His noisy companion seemed the more likely to be forthcoming with information, so, not surprisingly, Holmes turned his immediate attention to him. Initially no doubt, to put him at ease, Holmes asked him the most mundane, yet personal questions; such as his place of birth and his age. He was from Naples and he was just twenty three years old. Gialli clearly approved of Holmes's questioning technique, and he enthusiastically translated his every word, once the parrying was concluded and Holmes prepared his final thrust.

'Do hardship and poverty alone, justify your breaking of the law?' Holmes asked forcibly.

After much hesitation, Gialli finally extracted and communicated the blond prisoner's reply:

'I suppose it does not. Please, you must understand, the Doctor promised us much and vowed to protect us from the powers of the law!' The prisoner was clearly greatly agitated and Holmes's expression suddenly intensified at these last words. I could well understand why for one of the features of Moriarty's control of the underworld had been his vow and ability to protect his minions from punishment.

In more strident tones, Holmes asked his next question: ' 'The Doctor?' What Doctor is this? Is he your employer and benefactor?'

While the hapless blond was debating as to how best to answer, his companion suddenly threw off his cloak of indifference and attempted to silence him in a most animated fashion. However, his efforts were in vain. Holmes clearly had his colleague under his influence and the fellow seemed more taken by the idea of our assistance at his trial, than he was afraid of retribution from his 'Doctor'.

'I refer to the notorious Doctor Meyer, of Vienna, a most ingenious but dangerous man,' he nervously replied.

'Is he here in Rome, now?' Holmes next asked.

'No Signor. He keeps a small estate close to the ruins of Hadrian's villa, at Tivoli,' the man replied, clearly warming to his task.

'Describe Doctor Meyer to us, as fully as you can,' Holmes requested, now in a state of great excitement. He lit a cigarette while awaiting the prisoner's next reply. This was some while in coming, for the swarthy fellow was now babbling loudly, as one in fear of his very life, was eventually forcibly removed to enable us to continue. Gialli too, showed signs of impatience as he began to translate the laborious description. Finally we had a complete picture of the 'Doctor's' appearance and Gialli immediately arranged a landau for our journey to Tivoli.

Within moments we were hurtling along the streets of Rome, towards its northern suburbs, at break-neck speed. Despite our velocity, it promised to be a long journey, so I took this opportunity to read aloud the notes I had taken of Doctor Meyer's description, more for Holmes's benefit than Gialli's or my own. The words are my own précis, not those of our incoherent Neapolitan prisoner.

'Doctor Meyer is a very tall man, slim of build though encumbered with unusually rounded shoulders and a pronounced stoop to his back. His features, although partially obscured by an untidy grey beard, are sharp and lean. His lips are thin and his strange, penetrating eyes betray not a hint of the kindness one would normally expect to see in those of a man of medicine. His forehead positively protrudes with the great size of his brain and his head constantly oscillates from side to side, very much like that of a lizard. He is most awesome to behold,' the prisoner's statement concluded.

At these words, Holmes slapped his knee, with the palm of his hand, and turned excitedly towards me.

'I tell you Watson, take away the beard and we have our man! If our arrival at Tivoli is well timed, I may yet lay the ghost of my costly error of seven years ago.' Holmes returned to the window, urging the driver to ever greater speeds. It seemed to me, however, that any further increase in our pace would shake our vehicle to its very frame. Gialli evidently shared my sentiment, for his tiny moustache was constantly twitching and his grip on the handle on the door was turning his knuckles white.

At last, once we began to slow, I could see in the near distance the remarkably well preserved remains of Hadrian's spectacular villa through our carriage window and, shortly afterwards, we turned into a long, Cypress-lined drive-way.

At the end of the drive, we pulled up outside a building that was disappointingly modest, the more so when compared to its illustrious, ancient neighbour. The house was small and square, plain in design and white in colour. Its only allusion to the classical tradition being two undecorated pillars that flanked the main entrance.

The grounds were sadly neglected, the decor badly decayed and the pervading mood of the place was reflected in Holmes's crestfallen demeanour. It was now obvious that the place was unoccupied. A thorough search of each and every room confirmed this. Nobody, not even a groundsman, remained to inform us of the former occupant's current whereabouts. Our inquiries, at the local village and its railway station bore equally little fruit.

Holmes was clearly distraught and exclaimed: 'I have been a slow, dull-witted fool, Watson! As a consequence the most dangerous criminal mastermind of his age, is free to ply his evil trade once again! I suppose any small consolation I might extract from my failure, is that we have thwarted him, at least on this occasion and cleansed the city of Rome of his odious stench.'

'You have done more than any other man could possibly have achieved,' I ventured, by way of consolation. Gialli went further by offering him a large civic reception, a handsome reward and the city's highest honours. Typically, Holmes politely declined the reception, but his graciousness would not allow him to deal likewise with the medal of honour. Surprisingly, considering their many stark contrasts, Holmes and Gialli had built a strong bond of mutual respect and upon our final departure, theirs was a heart-felt farewell, during which Gialli vowed to inform us of any future incursion on his jurisdiction by Moriarty or his men.

Our journey home seemed slow and ponderous in comparison to our frantic outward dash. This had been so full of the anticipation of adventure and potentially a final confrontation with Holmes's nemesis. However, despite the anticlimactic cloud, that hung over us both, Holmes did make some attempt at engaging conversation and I admired him for that.

However, we both knew that Moriarty's latest defeat at our hands would undoubtedly spur him to future vengeance, the nature and timing of which, we could only speculate on.

THE END

Other titles in the
Linford Mystery Library:

THE FLUTTERING

David Whitehead

Something terrifying has started happening in Eggerton. People are turning up drained of blood and very, very dead. Have vampire bats started attacking humans? If so, then who's delivering the hammer-blow that finally kills the victims? For Detective Inspector Jack Sears it's a mystery that not even virologist Doctor Christopher Deacon can fathom. But then the police get lucky. Against all the odds one of the victims survives. But strangely enough, that's when things go from bad to worse . . .

DARK LEGION

John Glasby

Near the village of Tormount, on Cranston's Hill, Malcolm Amberley had been found dead. He was discovered in the centre of the Standing Stones, clutching the curiously ornamented hilt of a strange dagger, driven into his heart. A curtain of evil hung over the village, a nightmare for Terence Amberley who arrived to attend his brother's funeral. Did Malcolm commit suicide, or did some evil force still remain viable in the area, forcing him towards a mysterious death?